Also by Susanna Shore

Tracy Hayes, Apprentice P.I.
Tracy Hayes, P.I. and Proud
Tracy Hayes, P.I. to the Rescue
Tracy Hayes, P.I. with the Eye

Two-Natured London series

The Wolf's Call
Warrior's Heart
A Wolf of Her Own
Her Warrior for Eternity
A Warrior for a Wolf
Magic under the Witching Moon
Moonlight, Magic and Mistletoes

Thrillers

Personal
The Assassin

Contemporary Romances

At Her Boss's Command
It Happened on a Lie
To Catch a Billionaire Dragon
Which Way to Love?

Tracy Hayes, Apprentice P.I.

P.I. Tracy Hayes 1

Susanna Shore

Crimson House Books

Book Design: A. K. S. Keinänen
Cover Design: A. K. S. Keinänen

ISBN 978-952-7061-19-0 (paperback edition)
ISBN 978-952-7061-20-6 (e-book edition)

www.crimsonhousebooks.com

Chapter One

MY LIFE TOOK AN EXCITING turn on a hot August Tuesday. Mind you, I didn't appreciate my good luck when I found myself jobless and broke through no fault of my own.

Well, almost no fault of mine.

I was carrying a dog that smelled of puke, which didn't improve my mood. Not that it was the dog's fault he smelled. The poor thing had gorged on donuts and then thrown up everything.

That he'd snuck into the kitchen of Café Marina to eat the donuts I'd left unguarded—and then regurgitated them on the newly scrubbed floor—was the reason I was now jobless after sixteen months as a waitress there.

That he wasn't my dog hadn't saved me from being fired.

It was early afternoon and I was standing on the sidewalk outside the café, watching the busy traffic on Flatbush Avenue, Brooklyn, whizz past me, reeling from the fast turn of events. The 7th Avenue subway station was right across the street and I should've headed home, but my feet began carrying me in the opposite direction, clutching the dog against my chest like a stuffed toy for comfort. My head was spinning, and I felt sick to my stomach.

How the hell was I supposed to pay the rent without a job? I didn't have a penny to my name. I'd be homeless by the end of the month and have to move back in with my parents. They already thought I didn't know how to adult—at twenty-seven. I'd never hear the end of it.

Oh, they'd be sympathetic and understanding—this wasn't exactly the first job I'd lost these past six years—and then they'd ask my eldest brother Travis to find a suitable place for me—nothing too complicated, you understand. Or worse, they'd contact Aunt Moira, who worked in a canned soup factory. And I'd rather serve tables for the rest of my life than work there—which, admittedly, was the only profession I was good for with my skillset.

In fact, after six years of waitressing in various establishments around Brooklyn, I was a damn good waitress. Waitress extraordinaire.

Well, maybe I was exaggerating a little there.

But as dire as my financial situation was, I had more pressing concerns. "What should I do with you?" I cooed at the poor dog. He was listless after his bout of vomiting, but he licked my arm to show that he sympathized with my predicament, only he was just a little dog and had no idea either.

"My name is Tracy. Who are you?" I checked for his collar but he didn't have one. "Are you a stray?" But his coat was shiny and groomed. "You've run away, haven't you, you naughty boy?" The dog whimpered in answer. "Maybe you're someone's beloved pet and they're worried sick for you."

I paused when a thought hit. "Maybe they'll pay me to bring you back."

Having a purpose—however small—cleared my head. I retraced my steps and headed to the residential area behind the café with, if not actual spring in my step, then determined ambling, and started looking for missing dog posters. I wouldn't be too proud to take a fifty as a finder's fee. Moreover, Prospect Heights with its old townhouses was a neighborhood where only the rich could afford to live, so the finder's fee might even be substantial.

Then again: "You don't look like much though, do you?" Maybe he didn't belong to anyone wealthy after all.

The dog was more of a mongrel. At least he wasn't any breed I recognized, and I knew quite a few. I went through a dog phase when I was about ten, but to my eternal heartbreak I'd never had my own dog, because both my brothers were allergic to them. By the time I moved out on my own I'd got over wanting one. Never could afford it.

"What are you, a border terrier?" He had the build and looks of one: small, stocky body, longish, slim legs and a strong head with floppy ears. "But you've this nice, silky black and brown coat, so maybe some Yorkie in the mix?"

The dog didn't answer, and I hoped he wasn't getting sicker. I didn't know if donuts were deadly to dogs, like chocolate was, but it couldn't do him any good to eat a tray full of them, even if he had puked out most of it.

"You really should be more careful with what you eat, you know." If he was a pampered pet from around this neighborhood, he'd probably been fed with gourmet dog food. No wonder his stomach was upset.

Then again, dogs ate anything they found on the streets. Including dog poo. Donuts had to be an improvement.

I ambled—determinately—up and down the streets in the residential area, looking at lampposts for missing dog posters, but there weren't any. The dog probably hadn't been gone for long; he was in such a good condition. Maybe the owner would only miss him when he came home from work. But that would be a couple of hours from now.

"I can't carry you around that long," I said aloud.

But I didn't want to go home either. I lived in Midwood, a twenty-minute subway ride away, so not that far, but I only had enough on my MetroCard for one ride, and nothing to top it up with. I wouldn't be able to return if I left now.

"I'm not usually this bad off," I explained to the dog. He cocked an ear, so I was encouraged to continue. "But Jessica—my roommate for the past three years—moved in with her boyfriend two months ago, so now I have to pay the rent all by myself. And let me tell you, it's not easy with minimum wage plus tips."

Which I didn't have now either.

I was actually really miffed with Jessica for it. She just announced one day she'd be moving and was gone the next—and good luck asking her to contribute for last month's rent. She should've given me a warning at least, so I could've found a new lodger.

Moreover, I didn't want a new lodger. Jessica and I had got along well. Who knew what sort of idiot I'd had to put up with from now on just because I needed someone to pay half of the rent.

Actually, I couldn't even pay my half of the rent at the moment.

Of course, you could argue that I shouldn't have spent the last of my money on having my hair dyed, but it had been necessary. I have really mousy, mud-brown hair, an unfortunate genetic mix of my father's black-Irish hair—the kind with a hint of auburn in it—and my mother's strawberry blond. My sister Theresa—Tessa for short—had inherited beautiful auburn hair, but my auburn came from hairdressers. And it wasn't cheap, even though my hair only reached to my shoulders.

Anyway, vanity was the main reason I was now broke.

"Maybe I should take you to the police," I suggested to the dog when I spied the 78th Precinct's imposing limestone building on the corner of 6th Avenue. I had two cops in the family, and I tended to think cops could solve any problem I had.

But the dog gave a disgusted huff and I nodded. "Quite right. They'd only send us to Animal Control."

And I didn't know where the nearest one was—or have money to get there. Moreover, I didn't want to hand him to the nameless care of a shelter. I wanted to find the owner myself.

I wanted that finder's fee.

I turned towards Flatbush Avenue again, mostly because I'd covered the residential area already and didn't have any clear idea where to go from there. It was the closest main street, and I needed to find a place to sit. The August day was hot and the dog was a warm and surprisingly heavy bundle in my arms, making me even more uncomfortable, even though I was wearing my waitressing uniform of blue T-shirt and cute blue skorts, the kind that was shorts at the back and a skirt in the front, and flattering to my figure on both sides, though maybe I had slightly more figure around my bottom.

Marina Bellini, the owner of the café, had wanted me to leave the uniform before I left, but since I'd come to work wearing it, I couldn't very well leave naked.

"You'd better return it cleaned or I'll take it out of your last pay. And I'll most definitely deduct the donuts," she'd yelled after me as I was walking out the door. She had a fast and fierce temper, and while she cooled down fast too, I didn't doubt she meant what she said.

But at least I would be paid what was owed to me, so that was something to look forward to.

There was a Doughnut Plant at the corner of Bergen Street and Flatbush Avenue, and the mouth-watering scents wafting out from the kitchen door made the dog perk.

"Oh, no. No donuts for you. Ever," I said sternly, taking a tighter hold of him.

To be on the safe side I crossed the street and headed towards Atlantic Mall. At least it would be cooler there. A flock of people surged out from the Bergen Street station just as I passed the steps leading down. To avoid them, I walked closer to the wall, but that wasn't good either, because it brought me into the path of customers exiting a bank on the corner.

Swerving left and right, trying to avoid being trampled by busy Brooklynites, I walked smack into a stand placed on the sidewalk by the wall. The dog whined when I accidentally squeezed him as I tried to regain my balance, and I paused to soothe him. While at it, I read the advertisement on the stand.

Jackson Dean Investigations. Help wanted. Inquire on second floor.

My heart skipped a beat. A private investigator. Just what I needed. And they needed me too.

"Let's go in. I'm going to become a P.I."

Chapter Two

THE FIRST IMPRESSION OF THE building was pleasantly surprising. I associated private detective agencies with seedy back alleys and low-rent dives, but this was a block from the Barclay's Center on a fairly expensive stretch of a main street in Prospect Heights. The entrance hallway was—admittedly—worn, but the elevator at its end had been recently upgraded and everything was clean. The ride up was fast and soundless.

There were two doors on the second floor, one for a psychic—Madam Amber—of all things, and the other for Jackson Dean Investigations, as the nice brass plate on the door declared. The door was slightly ajar, so the dog and I went in.

We came into a small, windowless reception area with a dark brown hardwood floor and pale yellow walls. A desk for the secretary was on the right; a couple of chairs for customers to wait on were on the left, and wooden filing cabinets lined two walls. Judging by the papers and ring binders on the secretary's desk, the place was doing well. I gave the desk an apprehensive look, hoping it wasn't a secretary they were looking for.

Then again, anything beat waitressing.

Across the floor from the entry was a door with an opaque glass pane on it, and it was wide open. I had a clear view into the office, and the large hardwood desk in front of the windows. A man was sitting behind the desk, immersed in something on his computer screen. Since I couldn't very well keep standing there, holding the dog, I crossed the floor, but paused at the door to the office, not wanting to disturb the man.

The office was large and light. The windows looked over Flatbush Avenue and all its noise, but it wasn't terribly distracting. There were more filing cabinets and bookshelves here, chairs for clients in front of the desk, and a comfy couch wide enough for a man to sleep on at the side wall, with a wooden coffee table in front of it. Everything was slightly worn and mismatched, but clean and comfortable. I felt immediately at home.

But it didn't look like a P.I.'s office. Not that I was entirely sure what I'd expected. Magnifying glasses and a row of wigs for disguising oneself perhaps?

I gave the doorframe a knock and walked in. The man glanced up and drew back, baffled. "Who the hell are you?"

He had a pleasant voice, low and comfortable, the kind you'd want your priest to have. Though I was fairly sure Father Seymour would never say "Who the hell are you?"

Then again, I hadn't been to church in about a decade. Maybe he'd changed.

"Tracy Hayes. The reception was empty so I just came in."

He hurried to his feet, clearly thinking that I was a client, and rounded the desk to shake my hand, only to halt when he spotted my bundle. "Is that a dog?"

"It's under debate at the moment." I switched my hold of the dog under my left arm and offered my right hand to the man. He gave it a firm shake, his eyes on the dog.

"Jackson Dean."

He was in his mid-thirties, around five-eleven with long legs, and in really good shape with wide shoulders and sinewy arms that were bared by his black T-shirt. He looked great, but I'd imagined a fat middle-aged wash-out with a whiskey habit and a wheeze from a pack–a-day routine, so I didn't quite know how to relate.

Okay, fine, this was better.

He was wearing black jeans with his T, and black Converse sneakers, which gave him some edge without drawing attention to him. He had short, dark brown hair that wasn't quite out of shape yet even though it should have been cut a couple of weeks ago. And he had the kind of face you forgot the moment your back was turned—clean lines, pleasant, but unmemorable. In short, perfect for surveillance work.

Then he shot me a piercing look that made me upgrade my assessment of him.

He had the sharp, all-seeing eyes of a seasoned cop. I knew those eyes. My dad was a retired cop with an excellent glare, and my brother Trevor was a homicide detective working his way towards a good glare of his own. The look transformed Jackson's face completely. You wouldn't forget his face once you'd seen that look.

"What can I do for you, Miss Hayes?" he asked, taking a seat behind his desk. I sat on a chair in front of it, holding the dog.

"You had a sign downstairs saying you need help?" It came out as a question, but I couldn't avoid it. His eyes had unsettled me.

He studied me slowly. "You're not exactly what I had in mind."

My heart fell; it had really set its eyes on this job and had managed to get the rest of my body excited about it too.

"Really? I'd love to become a P.I."

His mouth quirked and lines appeared around his brown eyes, softening them. He didn't look so scary anymore. "It takes years of in-work experience and studying to become a P.I., if you're not a cop or a lawyer."

That was upsetting to hear, but I wouldn't give up so

easily. "I can learn," I said with more confidence than I felt. Studying of any kind wasn't exactly my ballgame.

"I'm sure you can, but I'm looking for someone tougher. You look like a nice home-girl."

"Was that an assessment of my looks or my age?" Because I wasn't that short to my weight at five six, and if my round parts were rounder than they'd been before I started working at the café, I wasn't a softie on the inside.

"Both, I guess," he said.

"I've been a waitress in Brooklyn for six years. They don't come tougher than that."

He laughed aloud, which banished the last effects of his stare. "Be that as it may, this job can be rough, and I'd like someone who can defend himself."

"My dad's a cop. I can defend myself."

Annnnd the piercing look was back. "Anyone I might know?"

"Sergeant Colm Hayes. He worked at the 66th. He's retired now."

He frowned, as if the name rang a bell. "I see." But he didn't elaborate. He leaned back in his chair, linked his hands behind his head, and proceeded to give me the third degree.

He wasn't impressed with my answers. I was too young, for one—which felt both good and insulting for someone who was twenty-seven already—and too poorly educated.

"You're saying you don't have any formal education, Miss Hayes?"

"I have a year in college." If I sounded defensive it's because I was. My three older siblings were over-achievers, and never forgot to remind me what I could have been if I'd stayed in college.

"Then what happened?"

It wasn't a story I shared easily, but since I didn't want him to think I was too stupid for college, I told him: "I thought it would be more important to follow the man of my dreams as he toured the country with his band than to get a degree."

"And was it?"

"Up until I caught him doing a groupie in the back-room of a concert venue." My stomach still roiled every time I remembered the scene, even though it was six years ago already. "Then it was a fast divorce and back to my parents."

"But not back to college?"

"I needed to clear my head first. And then I needed to save money for it." Neither of which had gone very well, but I wouldn't tell him that.

"And now it's just you and your faithful dog?"

I glanced at the dog, who had recovered enough to squirm on my lap, so I took a tighter hold of him. "He's not mine." The baffled look on his face was so comical I had to laugh. "I think he's run away."

He cocked a dark brow, prompting me to go on.

"He somehow got into the kitchen of the café I worked in." I considered. "Okay, maybe I should've kept a better eye on wandering strays when I took the donut delivery, but we were busy scrubbing the place because the health inspector was about to make a visit."

I'd also been busy ogling at the donut delivery guy. There were so few things that brought joy to a waitress's life and he was one of them. Donuts were the other, so he was pretty much the best thing in the world as far as that café was concerned. I could hardly be blamed for indulging.

But I wasn't going to tell Jackson that.

"I placed the box down for two minutes, and when I came back the dog had gone through it all."

The man looked impressed. "Not bad for a tiny dog."

"I know. If only he could've kept it in. But he threw everything up. At the feet of the health inspector."

Jackson threw his head back and barked a laugh. "Then what happened?"

"I was fired on the spot."

"That was a bit rash of your boss."

"She has a temper." Also I was late coming to work for the third time this month, but I thought it best not to share that piece of information either.

"What did you think to do with the dog?"

"Someone must miss him, so I figured I'll put up posters around the café and see if he's claimed."

He nodded. “Sounds like a plan. Why don’t you start with that and we’ll see from there.”

I straightened in the chair, excited. “I got the job?”

“I may regret this, but yes. For now.” He smiled. “Welcome to Jackson Dean Investigations.”

Chapter Three

MY DELIGHT MADE THE dog perk up. He jumped down before I could prevent him and proceeded to sniff around the office, his tail wagging in excitement. I took that as a sign that he had recovered, and since Jackson didn't seem to mind, I let him be.

"So what does the job entail?"

"Now you ask?" Corners of his eyes crinkled in amusement.

I shrugged. "It has to be better than waitressing."

"It depends on the assignment. But at least the days are usually shorter and hours are more flexible."

I liked the job already. Six years of ten hour days, seven days a week, had utterly worn me out.

"I take it there's enough work to take an apprentice?"

"Apprentice, huh?" Jackson teased me. "Yes, there is. Apart from my own clients, I do investigative work for the DA's office and the Brooklyn Defender Service."

The latter caught my interest, because Travis worked as a defense attorney there. "Sounds intriguing."

He shrugged. “It’s basic work: interviewing the witnesses, trying to come up with new evidence, going through people’s trash.” He added the last bit with a challenging smile, but I wouldn’t be intimidated. It couldn’t be worse than mopping dog vomit. Or human vomit for that matter; I’d done that too during my years as a waitress.

“Requires manpower and doesn’t pay too well.”

“And how much are you paying me?”

“I can’t pay you more than 10.50 per hour, I’m afraid.”

“It’s better than the 7.65 plus tips I earned as a waitress,” I said, impressed. Especially since the tips at the café hadn’t been all that great. “What else do I need to know?”

“There’s a lot of driving required. Do you have a car?”

“No.”

“Do you at least have a driver’s license?”

“I do. I just can’t afford a car.” I hadn’t really needed one in my line of work.

“How do you get around?”

“I have a MetroCard.”

He grinned. “That’ll have to do.”

I smiled too. “As long as the clients live within the reach of public transportation, I’m good.”

“Clients might, but I’m not so sure about the bad guys,” he said. “But you can always borrow my car if it comes to that.” That sounded nice.

“Or I can borrow my dad’s car.”

"Even better." Then he clapped his hands together. "Now, let's see if Cheryl's come back from the courthouse already."

We returned to the reception area sans the dog. He had jumped on the couch and was busy making a nest for himself on it, twirling around as if leveling hay or grass. Cheryl—who I assumed was the secretary—hadn't returned, so Jackson seated me at her desk and moved the mouse to make the computer screen wake up. A mugshot of a very ugly man, or possibly a warthog—the face was so scarred it was difficult to tell—came into view, and we both pulled back.

"Shouldn't be too difficult to find that one," Jackson muttered to himself as he opened an empty Word document for me. I could've done it myself, but he probably didn't want me messing around on his secretary's computer.

"Do you do skip tracing too?"

"Only when I'm bored. Keeps things interesting. Especially if I step on the toes of the big bounty hunters. That guy's free game though. Bonded by a small agency that doesn't have their own bounty hunters. They send cases my way occasionally."

I shuddered, thinking I'd have to chase after him, but didn't say anything. I wouldn't make much of a P.I. if I was frightened by the people I'd encounter.

And it wasn't as if I hadn't come across all sorts as a waitress.

"Do you know how to compose a missing dog poster?"

"Yes. I'm great at posters. I used to handle the advertising for my ex's band."

They hadn't exactly been in the Madison Square Garden league, more in the local saloon slash bar slash community center league. We did everything ourselves, including advertising. And since people usually found to the band's gigs, I was pretty sure my advertisements had worked.

Then again, they hadn't exactly flocked in to them.

"I'll leave you to it, then."

"Shouldn't I take a photo of the dog for the poster?"

"Better leave that out. Put 'released against accurate description' on it."

I looked at him baffled. "Why would anyone try to claim a dog that isn't theirs?"

"People are weird," he said with emphasis. "And for further measure, the owner should pay a good finder's fee, which should keep the wannabes out. Say two hundred?" My face lit up at the notion and he grinned. "I'll take my cut off it, of course."

I didn't care. It was infinitely better than what was in my pockets at the moment.

Cheryl hadn't returned by the time I'd composed and printed the posters, so—with a guilty look towards the closed door of Jackson's office—I made another ad, for a room to let. It was time I stopped moping over Jessica and her half of the rent and did something about it.

I'd just finished the ad—and deleted the incriminating document—when a short and round woman in her early fifties waltzed in. She stopped in her tracks when she saw me behind the desk, pulled up straighter, and puffed her cheeks. I recognized the fighting stance for what it was and immediately scooted back in the chair to make a fast escape. I was fairly sure I'd lose to her.

She had stuffed her voluptuous figure into a pink two-piece skirt suit and a black top with a plunging neckline that showed an impressive cleavage. Her face was heavily made up, and her blond hair was so recently done in a bouffant style I'd say her trip to the courthouse had probably included a visit to a hairdresser too.

"Who are you and what are you doing there?" she demanded to know.

I got hastily up as she marched towards me, the heels of her pink shoes clicking against the hardwood floor. She would deal with trespassers to her dominion with ruthlessness.

"I'm Tracy Hayes, the new apprentice."

She stopped in front of me, gave me a thorough once-over and sneered. "You're wearing a waitress's uniform."

I brushed my hand self-consciously down the side of my outfit. "I've made a recent career change."

"Very recent." She sat behind her desk and checked the computer. "Have you touched anything?"

"Only the Word document. I needed to make some posters for a dog I found."

"Starting your career with a bang, I see."

"At least it's a career."

Scratching on the other side of Jackson's door indicated that the dog was over his nap and wanted to know what was happening on this side of the door, so I let him out. He jumped enthusiastically around me, as if we were old friends, before heading to Cheryl to make her acquaintance. She crouched down to scratch his ears and a moment later they were best friends too.

"I'm Cheryl Walker," she said, appeased. "I look after this agency and that silly bastard over there." She nodded towards Jackson's office. I wouldn't have characterized him as silly—and I wouldn't dare to make assumptions on his parentage—but I nodded.

"He seems nice."

"Oh, he's the best."

I found her opinion of my new boss reassuring—not that I'd had reservations. I'd liked Jackson from the start.

"I need to go spread these posters. Would it be okay to leave the dog here until then?"

"Absolutely. We'll be fine here, won't we?" she cooed at the dog sitting on her lap. He licked her lips in answer. I shuddered and decided not to tell her that the dog had very recently vomited. Instead, I asked if she had a staple gun I could borrow. Armed with it, I headed out and to my first assignment as an apprentice P.I.

My step was positively buoyant when I returned an hour later. I'd spread the posters in the residential area nearby, and into all the cafés, restaurants, and shops in a two block radius, including the Atlantic Terminal Mall—but not Café Marina; I wasn't suicidal. I might not be a P.I. yet, or even much of an apprentice, but Tracy Hayes, apprentice P.I., sounded hell of a lot better than Tracy Hayes, unemployed waitress, or Tracy Hayes, college dropout. So I wasn't a defense lawyer like Travis, or an ER doctor like Tessa, or even a homicide detective like Trevor. But I was something.

While I'd been gone, Cheryl had popped out and bought a collar and a leash for the dog. Both were pink, because according to her, "He was secure enough to handle it."

He didn't seem to mind.

I was conflicted. It wasn't like I could've afforded them, and the dog definitely needed them. But he was slipping out of my care and I felt possessive of him. Our destinies were entwined. We belonged together.

But he had got me a new job, so I decided to be magnanimous.

"They look great. Do you think you'd be able to take care of him until the owner is found? I know nothing about dogs." It was a lie, but better than admitting I didn't have a penny to feed him.

"Oh, absolutely. We'll have such a wonderful time together, won't we?" The dog looked like he agreed, his tail wagging so fast I feared he would drop off Cheryl's lap, so I left them to bond and knocked on Jackson's door.

Chapter Four

"FIRST MISSION ACCOMPLISHED, boss," I said, taking a seat in front of his desk.

"In all fairness, it was an easy one."

"I don't know, those staple guns are tricky." I said it lightly, but I'd had a few annoying moments with it.

He grinned. "It's best not to arm you with a real one then."

"There are guns involved? Waitressing never involved guns."

If it did, there'd be a massacre practically every day when the harried staff dealt with that one customer who changed their mind five times and then complained when they didn't get what they'd ordered the first time and requested to see the manager.

"Not for you," he said sternly.

"I know how to shoot." Dad had made all of us learn.

Then again, I'd never been very good at it. Guns were loud and smelly, and I hadn't liked shooting all that much. I hadn't touched any kind of weapon in years, so it was perhaps best I wasn't armed.

"I don't doubt it. I recognized your father's name, so I checked your background to make sure it was the same man. I used to know your family well."

"You did? Were you a friend of Travis's?"

My brothers' friends used to fill the house when I was a kid, but they were eight and four years older than me, so I didn't pay any attention to them—other than finding them a nuisance. By the time I was old enough to take interest in boys, my brothers had already moved away, emptying the house of their friends too. Jackson was about Travis's age, and I'd been ten years old when Travis's friends stopped coming over, so it wasn't a wonder that I had no recollection of him.

"Yes. Travis and I went to school together and he always welcomed me to your home. I think I even remember you as a scrawny little girl with pigtails," he added with a smile. I had been scrawny, but if he remembered the pigtails, I must've been really small.

"And Trevor and I worked briefly in the same precinct when I was a homicide detective."

"I knew you'd been a cop," I said, pleased with myself.

"How so?"

I had a notion he didn't ask just out of curiosity, but to test me. "You've cop's eyes."

He looked mildly impressed with the answer. "That's the kind of attention to detail I'm hoping for from you. That a waitress would be good at reading people—even if you don't have any obvious qualifications for the job."

"If I were, I'd never have married my bastard of an ex."

"We learn from our mistakes."

We certainly did, which meant a century-long dry spell for me when it came to dating of any kind.

"There are some formal things you have to learn pretty fast though. Your rights and what you can and can't do, those sort of things." He picked a stack of printed papers from his desk and handed them to me. "Read these for a start."

"Will there be a test?" I eyed the papers in dismay. Already the title page made my eyes water with its official language.

"Absolutely."

I'd only asked as a joke, but now a lump settled into my guts, like every time a test was mentioned. But I could do this. I'd survived as a waitress; I could read a few legal papers.

"You'll also need an ID. Look here."

I did and he took my photo with a huge camera he'd pulled out of nowhere before I could so much as blink. He checked the result from the display and grinned.

"That'll do."

"Hey!"

Ignoring my protest, he uploaded the photo to his computer and printed it, while I combed my hair with my fingers, as if it would help at this point.

"Sign here."

Jackson gave me a two-by-three cardboard card with the official information of his firm printed on it. He had already filled it in with my name and other required information, and I signed on the appointed line. He took the card and went to a side desk where he had printers and other machines, took the photo from the photo printer and attached it to the card. Then he laminated the thing before giving me the finished product.

"There. Now you're officially in my employment."

I stared at the card, delighted. Yes, the picture was horrible, but no more so than on my driver's license. Wisps of hair were shooting everywhere, and I had a slightly shell-shocked expression in my blue eyes, but you could recognize me from it. More importantly, it meant authority that I'd never had before.

"I'm a licensed P.I.!"

"No, you're an employee of a licensed P.I. There's a vast difference," Jackson said sternly, but I didn't really care.

"What's next, boss?" I couldn't wait to get to show the ID to everyone.

"Next you'll fill out all these employment forms." When I groaned he smiled. "And then we'll call it a day."

It was closing time by the time I'd filled out the forms. Cheryl was already leaving with the dog when I dropped the forms on her desk, and I spent a moment petting him. He really was the cutest little thing.

"I'll miss him." I didn't care anymore that I'd been fired—because of him. It really had been a blessing in disguise. I had a good feeling about my new job.

"I'll bring him back tomorrow," Cheryl said cheerfully. She was so happy about the dog that I feared the separation would be hard on her when we found the owner.

"We should give him a name to call him by while he's with us."

"You name him," she said magnanimously.

I didn't have to think. "Pippin. From the *Lord of the Rings*. He's small, cute, and he likes to eat, just like the hobbit Pippin."

"Pippin he shall be, then." And she was out the door with a wave of her hand, her heels clicking, Pippin following her smartly on his pink leash.

I was slower to leave and Jackson caught me at the elevator.

"Do you need a ride home?"

"If it's not out of your way," I said, delighted. That way I could save my one MetroCard ride for the morning.

"I'm headed to Kensington for an assignment."

"My parents live there!" Maybe I could borrow Dad a twenty to top my card with.

He smiled. "I know. I spent a lot of time in your house when I was growing up, remember."

I raked my brain for any recollection of him, but the boys had all looked the same to me. "You were good friends with Travis?"

"Anything beat my home."

I didn't know what to say to that.

Jackson drove a ten-year-old, steel gray Toyota Camry sedan. It was the kind of car that fit in everywhere without drawing attention—much like the owner himself. He seemed to have an eye for details like that.

"It's cleaner than I expected," I noted, eyeing the interior of the car. "I thought it would be littered with fast food wrappers and empty soda cans."

He smiled. "You caught us on a good day. I've just had her cleaned."

"What made you choose to become a cop?" I asked when we were on our way, infinitely curious.

"It was either that or a life of crime."

"You don't look like an ex bad boy." I kept my tone light to hide my surprise.

"Looks can be deceiving."

They certainly could. And I was beginning to think his were deliberately so.

Rush hour was heavy, but Jackson seemed to know all the less congested streets and it took us only a little over half an hour—for the fifteen minute ride—to reach Kensington. It was a long and narrow neighborhood in the middle of Brooklyn, a nice old working class residential area that hadn't been gentrified yet, with mixed demographics and safe streets.

My parents lived on the East 4th Street in a typical one-family foursquare from the early 20th century. It was a white clapboard, high and narrow, with a porch and a tiny yard in the front, with bushes and flowerbeds that mother took pride in, and a slightly larger yard at the back. A living room, a dining room and a kitchen downstairs, and four small bedrooms upstairs—Tessa and I had had to share until Travis moved away from home. With one bathroom, it was like all the other houses there, small, functional, and cozy. And every time I visited I was struck anew with wonder: how the hell had we all fit in there?

Jackson pulled over outside the house without instructions from me. "It looks exactly the same as it did—" He paused to calculate: "Seventeen years ago when I was here last."

I gave the house a fond look. "I know." Then I hesitated. "Would you like to come to dinner? There's always plenty."

"I have fond memories of your mom's cooking," he reminisced.

"It's Dad cooking these days. He got bored after he retired and learned to take care of the household."

He looked impressed. "If you're sure I'm not intruding."

"No one's ever intruding in our house. But Dad's cooking can be a bit ... experimental." This made him laugh.

I led him in and to the kitchen at the back of the house, where we found Dad. He was still the same handsome Irish devil he was in their wedding photo, tall and straight-backed, even if there was softness around his bright blue eyes that hadn't been there when he was on active duty, and his dark hair had turned gray.

"Smells great," I said by way of greeting, making him smile.

"What brings you home in the middle of the week, pumpkin?" He gave me a hug and noticed Jackson. "Who's this, then?" He frowned. "You're Jackson ... Dean, aren't you?"

Jackson offered Dad his hand and they shook. "Well remembered, sir." I was impressed too, but then again, Dad had an adult's view to the children who had swarmed in his house. Moreover, as a cop, he had necessarily needed a good memory for faces.

"You were a bit of a handful, if I recall," Dad said.

"I grew out of it."

"Jackson's a P.I. now and he's my new boss. I'm the apprentice P.I. in his detective agency."

This brought the full force of Dad's impressive—and knee-shaking—stare on me. "What?" He didn't look at all delighted by my news, which surprised me a little. He had never liked me waitressing. I told him about my day.

"But a P.I., Tracy? Are you sure? It can be a really rough job," he said, his graying brows furrowing in worry.

"I'm fairly sure Jackson won't give me anything I can't handle at first."

Before Dad could argue more, Mom came home and we sat to dinner. She was a shorter and curvier version of me—or rather I was a taller and leaner version of her—except that she had nice strawberry blond hair and green eyes, and I had Dad's blue eyes. She was a nurse at a nearby maternity clinic, a regular nine-to-five job she'd had for as long as I could remember. And if you think that being surrounded by babies all day long had made her immune to wanting grandchildren, you'd be wrong.

Her eyes lit up when she saw Jackson and I knew the look. She hoped that I had—at long last—brought a nice man to meet them. I hated to disappoint her, but I had learned my lesson. There would never ever again be a nice man I'd introduce them to.

She hid her disappointment when she learned who Jackson was, but not about me losing another job. She took a practical view, however. "It's not like you can keep it more than six months."

"Hey! I stayed at the Café Marina for over a year," I said, offended.

"And that truly is a miracle."

"It's not my fault I was fired from those other jobs."

"It never is."

I glanced at Jackson to see how he took that, but he just smiled. "Thank you for the dinner. It was excellent," he said to Dad, and looked like he meant it, even though the gravy had been lumpy and much too salty. “I’m afraid I have to go to work now.”

“Can I come too?”

I shot up without waiting for his answer. Wherever he was headed, it had to be better than an evening with my parents, watching their disappointed faces and being lectured about my life choices.

Chapter Five

TEN MINUTES LATER WE WERE back in Jackson's car. I was dressed in my jeans I'd forgotten at my parents' and one of Mom's T-shirts—I couldn't very well go on an assignment in my waitressing uniform—and armed with a thermos of coffee and sandwiches Mother had made us. Jackson eyed them with delight.

"It's nice to have someone looking after you."

That sounded lonely. "If only they wouldn't meddle with my life otherwise."

"You can't cherry pick with families," he said mildly, but I detected a bitter undertone. He probably hadn't had a nice childhood if he'd been on a path to juvie. I really wanted to pry, but I'd only just met him.

I'd ask Travis.

"What's the job?" I asked instead.

"A husband thinks his wife is having multiple affairs while he's gone, so I'm keeping an eye on their house."

"Multiple, huh? What happened to regular affairs?"

Jackson smiled. "So far I haven't seen any men go

into the house, and this is the second time the husband's been away from town. I'm beginning to think he's imagining the whole thing."

Our target was one street over and a half a street down from my parents', and I knew the house well. A grandfather of a friend of mine had lived there before he'd moved to Florida a couple of years ago, when house prices started to rise in this area. It was narrower than my parents' house and painted red in a past so distant it had faded to pink.

"I see the new owners have done nothing with the place," I noted. Jackson made to pull over a couple of houses down the street, but I prevented him.

"Not here. Mrs. Bradshaw who lives in that house will call the cops if a strange car is parked outside her house for more than ten minutes."

Jackson grinned, but chose another spot. "You've proven yourself useful already."

I tried to hide my pleasure, but probably failed.

"Surveillance in a nice neighborhood like this can actually be trickier than in a shady one," he noted when he had parked the car. "People here pay attention to strangers."

"Hence the car that fits everywhere."

He smiled. "You noticed."

It was close to seven, but the sun wouldn't set for a while yet and there was enough light to keep an eye on the house from a distance. There wasn't a car in the driveway, so either Mrs. Jenkins, the wife, wasn't home, or she had parked on the street.

"Curtains are drawn," I noted. "Highly suspicious in this neighborhood at this hour."

"She should be home. She works as a pediatrician at the University Hospital of Brooklyn. Nine to five hours."

"Tessa is an ER doctor there!"

"She's a doctor? I always thought she'd become a supermodel." He had that dreamy look in his eyes men always got when they thought of my gorgeous sister. I was used to it and didn't mind.

Much.

"She actually put herself through college and med-school by modeling."

All my older siblings had paid for their education with scholarships and work. I didn't have accomplishments or skills that would've merited a free education, so my parents had had to pay for mine, but since I'd only done one year in college, it hadn't been that straining for them. And I intended to pay them back one day.

"That's impressive."

It was, but it hadn't done my self-confidence good that it had been constantly pointed out to me when I was a gangly and insecure teenager. Mostly by aunts and uncles, though; not by my parents.

We settled to wait. The sun set and it started to become dark, but there was no movement in or out of the house. Light shone through a crack in the curtains, however, so Mrs. Jenkins was home. I wouldn't have minded chatting, but Jackson had withdrawn into some sort of zone where he barely registered the outside world, his eyes trained on the target. I didn't dare disturb him, even though I had tons of questions. Like, where had he learned to do that, and could I learn too? My guess was in the military. Maybe he'd been a sniper. I'd heard they were trained to do that.

At some point I opened the thermos, which roused him, and we had the coffee and sandwiches. "If you were looking for excitement, this is pretty much it," Jackson said, smiling. "Stakeouts can be mind-numbing."

"I get to sit down and have coffee, and no one's harassing me. It's already better than waitressing."

The last light had faded when a car finally pulled over outside the pink house. Jackson lifted his camera to take a look through its long lens. A woman exited the car dressed in a sleek, dark pantsuit, and high-heels that were unnecessary for someone as tall as her. She was easily six foot tall in them, but she didn't slouch a bit.

"I think it's the same woman who visited Mrs. Jenkins yesterday, but it was too dark to see her face clearly then too," Jackson said, annoyed.

The woman took an overnight bag from the back seat of her car and walked to the door of the pink house with a practiced ease that told me she was accustomed to wearing heels. Mrs. Jenkins opened the door and the two women were briefly illuminated by the light coming from the foyer behind her. Jackson fired the camera a couple of times, and the women disappeared indoors. Jackson checked the photos and shook his head.

"Nothing."

"Can't we go closer and see if we couldn't get photos through a crack in the curtains?"

"That would be illegal, I'm afraid."

"P.I.'s do that all the time in movies."

"We're not in a movie. And besides, we're here to prove that Mrs. Jenkins is having an affair."

I gave him a slow look he probably didn't see in the dark, so I used my sarcastic voice: "And she couldn't possibly be having an affair with a woman?"

Jackson pulled up straight, stunned. "What?"

I shook my head, amazed at his amazement. "A woman wouldn't receive a sister or a friend dressed in a negligee that barely covered her lady bits. And the other woman was carrying an overnight bag."

"But she's married to a man."

"Like that's never happened before. Either she's found herself later, or was afraid to come out and married just to keep up appearances."

Jackson was quiet for a few moments and then snorted out a laugh. "Mr. Jenkins is in for the surprise of a lifetime."

"Provided we can prove it."

Lights came on in the upstairs bedroom. "If you're right, I don't think they'll emerge until morning. There's nothing we can do here tonight." He started the car. "I'll drive you home."

"Drop me at my parents' instead. I need to let them know I'm fine."

Trevor was watching a *CSI* rerun on TV in the living room when I got in. At thirty-one, he still lived home, because he said he couldn't afford a place of his own, but I think he just liked having someone to cook and clean for him. Besides, this was an easy distance from his precinct.

He was a taller and more broad-shouldered and muscled version of Mom, with her strawberry blond hair—neatly cut—green eyes, and a fair complexion lightly dusted with freckles. I didn't have freckles, and his stronger features made him quite handsome, but you would never mistake us for anything but siblings. He'd got his education by way of the Marine Corps and a stint in Iraq, after which he'd become a cop. He'd been a plainclothes homicide detective for a little over a year now, and he loved his job.

"Don't you get enough of that stuff at work?" I asked as I slumped on the couch next to him.

"This is comic relief," he said, reaching out to pull me into a hug and then mess my hair with his knuckles as if we were still children. "Are you staying the night?"

"No, I just came to tell Mom and Dad that I'm okay and heading home."

"I'll give you a lift."

I'd hoped for it, because public transportation between my home and my parents' was so lousy it was practically nonexistent. A few minutes later we were in Trevor's black Ford Edge, driving towards Midwood, a neighborhood next to Kensington, with leftovers from dinner and my waitressing uniform, freshly washed and still warm from the dryer.

"Dad says you're working for Jackson Dean as a P.I. now."

"Is that derision I detect in your voice?"

"Not at all." But I could see his mouth quirk. "Only slight amusement. What brought that about?"

"I saw his ad and thought I'd be great."

"I'm sure you will."

"Thanks." I decided to take his words at a face value, despite his amusement.

"What do you think of the guy?"

I gave it a thought. "He's nice, but slightly intimidating, and seems to know his job. Why did he quit policing?"

"He was in homicide, and this job can get really stressful. When his partner got shot in the line of duty, he decided he'd had enough. He inherited the agency from an uncle around the same time, so I think it was an easy choice."

There was definitely more to my new boss than met the eye.

Trevor pulled over outside my building and leaned

over and kissed my cheek. "You'll do fine in your new job, little sister, don't worry. Now, do you have everything you need?"

I almost said yes. I didn't want to admit I had used up all my money, but I couldn't afford the pride. "Actually, could you lend me a twenty? I'm all out and it'll take a few days before I get my last paycheck from the café."

He dug out his wallet and gave me two twenties. "Here. Ask for more if you need."

"Thanks, big bro, but I'm sure I'll be fine."

I exited the car and he waited until he saw me enter the building. Jackson was right: it was nice to have someone looking out for me, even if they occasionally irritated me. So I blew Trevor a kiss before I disappeared indoors.

Chapter Six

I LIVED IN A SEVEN STORY REDBRICK from the 90s at the corner of Avenue J and Ocean Avenue, only two blocks away from Brooklyn College—not that I'd lived here when I did my one year there. It was a nice building with a live-in janitor that could be trusted to fix a leaking faucet, clean up the hallways, and keep out unsavory characters. It smelled of cleaning detergent, exotic spices, and cabbage. My neighbors all seemed to be able to cook the dishes of their native countries and did so regularly—or when they got homesick. But best of all, it was rent stabilized.

My apartment was on the fifth floor. It had two small bedrooms, a nice bathroom, and a kitchen-living room combo. Jessica and I had furnished the common area together and she had left most of the furniture for me when she moved away, because Harris, her boyfriend, already had everything. It was an eclectic collection of old pieces we'd got from relatives and found at the Salvation Army thrift store, very 70s chic: strong colors, easy to clean, and durable. It was my first own home—my scumbag of an ex and I had never got around to starting one, because we'd been touring with his band—and I loved it.

I was home earlier than most evenings, and the day—at least the latter part of it—had been lighter than normal, but I was utterly beat. I barely managed to do my evening wash-up before I dropped on my bed. I was instantly out.

I woke up when Mrs. Pasternak, my next door neighbor, banged on my bedroom wall from her apartment and yelled that I'd be sorry if the alarm went off one more time, because her son Olek, who was a baggage handler at JFK, had been on a night shift and needed his sleep. Apparently misdirecting luggage was an all-night operation.

I got up bleary-eyed and thankful. Jessica used to make sure that I woke up in time, and I'd been having significant trouble with it since she'd moved out. Checking the time I panicked. I'd slept half an hour too long without reacting to the alarm at all. No wonder Mrs. Pasternak was annoyed, if she'd had to listen to it beep that long. But then I remembered I didn't have to be at work until nine. I hadn't changed the wake-up time in my alarm before I went to bed, so it woke me up at six. Or tried to, anyway. Groaning in pleasure, I sank back to bed.

I startled awake half an hour later.

I shot up and prepared myself for work. It was nice to

actually choose what to wear instead of putting on a uniform—but more difficult than I remembered, especially since I didn't really have much clothes. It would be another hot day, so I selected a powder pink T-shirt—it slightly clashed with my hair, but I didn't care—and my only pair of summer pants—white but miraculously clean, tight and really good for my figure as they squeezed the extra bits in. My look didn't exactly match Jackson's black on black, but I felt great. At the back of my closet I found an old canvas messenger bag that would be perfect in my job. I'd fill it with everything I needed.

Breakfast was cereal without milk, because it had gone off and I'd forgotten to buy more. I began looking for a pen to compose a note for Jessica about it, only to remember she didn't live here anymore, and then spent a few moments wallowing in self-pity.

Despite the extra sleep, I was early to leave to work, so I made a detour by the college on my way to the subway. I needed a new housemate and I'd decided that the university was my best bet. I put the ad I'd made the previous day on the notice board by the housing office and crossed my fingers. It was almost a month until the next term started, but I felt confident someone would notice it before that. And if not, I'd manage the rent somehow until then.

Subway train was much more crowded than what I was used to and the people were different. This was the commute time for nine-to-five workers that I'd never been part of before. I found it exciting, even if it was hot in the car. It was a reminder that my life was different now.

I exited at my usual station—on purpose, not because I'd had forgotten; I'd never forget I had a new job now. I emerged onto 7th Street and crossed to Café Marina behind a group of commuters eager to get their morning lattes and muffins, and waited in line until it was my turn to be served. The surprised look on my former fellow waitress's face when she recognized me was worth the queueing.

"What are you doing here?" Kelly asked so loud that the entire café silenced for a second.

"Getting my morning latte and returning this." I showed her the uniform I'd packed neatly in a plastic bag.

"Couldn't you have taken it straight to the kitchen?"

"I don't have a key to the back door anymore."

"Well, I don't have time to serve you," she snapped. "Thanks to you, we're short-staffed this morning."

Hearing they were having a hard time without me pleased me. "I'm not the one who decided to fire me for something I didn't do." People behind me were getting impatient that the line wasn't moving, so I stepped aside and made a beeline for the kitchen door behind the counter. "I'll take this myself."

Lisa, another morning-shifter, was busy filling trays with donuts. "About time you showed up," she spat when she spotted me.

"I'm not staying. I was fired, remember."

"I'm sure Marina has calmed down by now."

"Possibly, but I haven't."

I walked past her to the back of the kitchen, where my erstwhile boss had her small office. It spoke volumes of her character that she wasn't at the counter helping Kelly, even though they were a staff short, but I didn't have to care about it anymore. I gave the open door a knock and entered.

"You!" She definitely hadn't forgiven me yet. She was Italian in both looks and temper.

"I came to return my uniform and collect my wages." I placed the plastic bag on her desk.

"I haven't calculated them yet."

"I can wait." I leaned against the doorjamb like I had all the time in the world.

"Fine." She pulled out her lists with my hours on them and began to add them up. "You know, you'd get a full two weeks' pay if you stayed and helped today."

"Thanks, but I already got another job."

Her mouth pressed into a line and she didn't say another word, not even to ask where I was working now. I itched to tell her, but I wouldn't volunteer the information, so it frustrated me a little when she kept her silence. She filled the necessary lines in her accounting program and a moment later her printer spewed out a check for me.

"I deducted the donuts."

"For their retail price, I see." But I wouldn't make a number of it. I had a check for almost eight hundred dollars. That was half of the rent covered. Eating was overrated anyway. Then again, I'd had to slave for nearly 140 hours for it. I should have more to show for it.

Even with my detours, I reached the elevator at the agency's building at the same time as Cheryl and Pippin. She was dressed in the same pink suit as the previous day, with a leopard print top underneath, and Pippin had a pink bow on his head. He was ecstatic to see me.

"He's not a guard dog, that's for sure," I noted, making Cheryl smile.

"He's a cutie, that's what he is."

We reached our floor and stepped out of the elevator just as Jackson emerged from the stairs, dressed in all black again, with a black blazer on, even though it was going to be another hot day. Then I caught a glimpse of a handgun in a shoulder holster and didn't wonder about the jacket anymore.

He gave me a baffled look, as if he'd forgotten he had hired me. Or possibly for my summery clothes. "You're early," he said, opening the office door and switching off the alarm.

"For me this is late." I followed him in to start my first proper day as an apprentice P.I.

It wasn't a terribly exciting morning, to be honest, but I enjoyed every moment of it. For the first time ever I was paid to sit on a nice couch with a cup of coffee and read. I definitely needed the coffee, because the reading was fairly dull. Jackson worked on his computer.

"Do you have interesting cases open?"

"Not anything high-profile. I recently finished a case for the DA against a drug lord. It's coming to trial this week."

"Was it dangerous?"

"No, but time-consuming and huge. The DA managed to bring down pretty much the entire operation along with the leader."

"So it's not solely about photographing cheating spouses?"

His mouth quirked. "Not solely. But how are your photography skills?" I had to admit my ignorance and he added lessons in it to my schedule—as well as buying a camera and a new phone for me on his shopping list.

"What's the phone for?" Not that I had anything against a new smartphone I didn't have to pay for.

"Let me count the ways... "

Turned out, a good smartphone was essential for a P.I. You could access all sorts of databases with it on the go, like most wanted, missing persons, and the DMV. Plus it had maps and a camera too.

"You never know when you need to have a license plate checked." He glanced at his watch. "Actually, we have time for shopping right now. Let's go."

So we went.

Chapter Seven

LESS THAN AN HOUR LATER we emerged from the Atlantic Terminal Mall after a whirlwind shopping excursion. Jackson knew exactly what he wanted and where he wanted it from; there was no window shopping, and God help the salesperson who tried to persuade him into buying what he didn't want. It was very effective, but not much fun.

I didn't mind. I was a proud owner of a new smart-phone, but not the camera. Jackson had decided that until I learned how to take photos with one of those long lenses—you needed them for stealth, long-distance photographing—I'd have to settle with one of his old cameras. I also got a notepad and pens that made me feel nostalgic for school for some reason.

"Do we have time to pop into that bank?" I asked, spotting my branch across the street.

"Of course. Why?"

"I'm carrying a check for eight hundred bucks in my bag."

To the surprise of no one, Jackson quick-marched me there.

It was almost lunch time, and those who had snuck out early from work to run errands were filling the small lobby, looking impatient for having to stand in line. Jackson eyed them in dismay.

"You know, you could handle this with an app on your new phone too," he said as I made my way to the desk at the side, where they had the depositing envelopes.

"It's not operational yet, is it." I wouldn't admit it aloud, but I didn't entirely trust those apps. It was much better to fill the envelope, which really didn't take that long, and push it through the appointed slot. Much more satisfying too.

"Now what?" I asked, my check safely in the care of the bank.

"Now lunch. Then we'll take care of your personal security. You have to be able to defend yourself if you plan on walking around with checks in your bag."

I refrained from telling him it wasn't exactly an every-day occurrence, and just followed him to lunch. I was even able to buy my own, thanks to Trevor. And the novelty of having lunch at a leisurely pace—sitting down—wouldn't wear off soon.

Jackson chose a small place behind the mall, and since it was near the 78th Precinct, the place was filled with cops. They all knew Jackson—partly because the agency was only a block away from the precinct, partly because he had a good reputation—and he was greeted like one of them. My presence caused some glee, especially when they learned I was his apprentice.

"What can she do? Check the ladies toilets for cheating spouses?"

I rolled my eyes. "As if there aren't any women police," I said to the sexist ass, a man about my age wearing a uniform. He only grinned.

"Not as fine as you."

I didn't know if I should be pleased or not. I wasn't exactly complimented every day, even though customers at the café had liked to flirt with the waitresses, but the tone it was given was disparaging.

Jackson came to my rescue. "I've seen your partner, O'Hara. She might get mad if she heard you say that." Everyone laughed, O'Hara included.

A detective in a rumpled suit came to our table. He was in his late forties, short and overweight with a receding hairline and a cigarette behind his ear, matching my image of what a P.I. should look like exactly. Jackson introduced him as Detective Lonnie Peters and we shook hands. He refrained from making asinine comments about my presence or gender, and just talked to Jackson.

"I hear you did a great job on the MacRath case." He smiled, but I detected an irritated undertone. Had it been his case? Cops could be territorial. "Congratulations."

"Thanks. I hope the streets are cleaner for a while."

"He didn't deal for street users. It was CEOs and rock stars for him, and someone will soon fill that vacancy."

Jackson admitted it with a grim nod. I was curious, but I deduced it was about the case Jackson had done for the DA. I felt proud of him.

After lunch we got into Jackson's car. He took Atlantic Avenue, a busy road that cut Brooklyn from west to east, heading east through the better neighborhoods of Crown Heights and Bedford and Stuyvesant. But we were almost in Brownsville—the opposite of a good neighborhood—before he pulled over outside a small strip mall. A fast food place on the right, women's clothes in the middle, and the store we were here for on the left.

Feeling apprehensive, I followed him into the store that specialized in private security business, everything from weapons to alarms and surveillance systems.

"I'm not getting a gun, am I?"

"No, but you do need protection, and not solely for those checks either. Your father is right. This job comes with its own set of hazards. You have to be prepared."

He proceeded to walk up and down the aisles, checking the merchandize with a keen eye. Now he was in a shopping mood. I followed with less enthusiasm.

Twenty minutes later I was the owner—with ambivalent feelings—of a pair of police quality handcuffs and a can of pepper spray. Jackson would've bought me a Taser too, but you needed a license for it, which gave me a good reason to refuse. With my luck, I'd manage to stun myself.

We were about to exit the shop when a man at a side counter showcasing handguns caught my attention, mostly because he was trying really hard not to be noticed. He had a baseball cap pulled low over his face but I recognized him instantly. Hard not to with that face.

I halted Jackson by placing a hand on his arm and leaned closer to him. "Behind your right shoulder is the ugly skip whose photo was on your computer yesterday."

Jackson didn't even twitch a brow, but just casually checked the direction I indicated. "You're right. Well spotted," he said in a low voice. "Wait here, I'll go get him."

I didn't want to miss the action on my first day, but I wouldn't be much use in making an arrest. So I walked to the exit instead and placed myself in front of it, proud of my initiative.

Jackson approached the man from the side, reaching behind his back for handcuffs I hadn't even noticed he had hidden under his blazer. He was about to announce himself when things went wrong.

The security guard had noticed the guy too, probably because he looked suspicious as hell with his ball cap pulled over his face. He walked straight toward the fugitive, not even pretending to hide his intentions. And why would he? It was his job to get rid of suspicious people loitering around guns.

Just as Jackson reached to take a hold of the skip's shoulder, the guy spotted the guard and instantly bolted for the door, managing to push Jackson off balance as he turned. A heartbeat later the only thing standing between him and freedom—was me.

I'd like to say I did something brave, like stood firm and yelled "Stop, you're under arrest," and then pulled a fancy move that stopped the fleeing guy in his tracks. Or that I'd at least fired the pepper spray that was in my hand.

But I didn't. I froze in horror as two hundred pounds of angry and desperate man barreled at me, his eyes so fixed on the door he barely noticed me there when he bowled over me. I flew backwards and landed heavily on my back, wind knocked out of my lungs, but by sheer luck I didn't bang my head.

"Are you all right?" Jackson's face appeared over mine, looking worried.

"Yes. Go," I wheezed.

He didn't wait for another command and disappeared out of the door, leaving me to pull myself together on my own. Helpful hands reached to assist me, and a moment later I was on my feet, swaying only a little.

"Are you all right? What happened?"

I gave the cashier who had asked the question my best reassuring smile I'd honed over the years. "We're private investigators. He's a fugitive who missed his court date."

The girl didn't look terribly surprised to hear it. "We get all kinds here."

The security guard returned, having run after Jackson and the fugitive. He wasn't exactly in the prime of his youth so he was panting heavily. "They got away." He fixed his eyes on me, but the look was mild compared to my dad's or Jackson's and I had no trouble keeping calm. "What do you know about this?"

I fished out my new ID from my bag and showed it to him. An excited thrill ran down my spine for the novelty of it. "Private investigators. That man was an FTA." 'Failure to appear', if you will, which I'd only that morning learned from the papers Jackson made me read, but I used it like a pro. "We were trying to arrest him when he fled." *Because of you*, I wanted to say, but I managed to keep that to myself. No need to upset him.

He looked pleased. "I knew there was something wrong with the guy."

"Yes, well spotted. Now, which way did they go?"

I had a mosquito's chance in an insecticide factory of catching them, but I jogged off in the direction the guard had pointed, trying not to limp. I'd fallen on my bag, which had softened my landing, but I'd still have a bruise on my tailbone. I kept running till I rounded the corner—not very far—and then I had to pause to catch my breath. I'd have to start exercising if I wanted to keep this job.

Now there was an aspect of my new life I wasn't particularly looking forward to.

Chapter Eight

I WAS LEANING AGAINST THE CAR when Jackson returned twenty minutes later—without the fugitive. He looked like a storm on two feet, so I decided not to ask any questions and just got in the car. The drive back to the agency went in silence.

My arrival gave Cheryl a fit. "Look at you," she shrieked. "What's happened?" Pippin jumped around me yapping, alarmed by Cheryl's tone. Jackson marched straight into his office and threw the door closed behind him so hard I feared the glass would break.

I took stock of my appearance as I sank down on one of the visitors' chairs—carefully, wincing when my tailbone protested. My summer pants were no longer white, but nothing was broken and I wasn't bleeding.

"We ran into a fugitive. Literally."

I told her the story and she immediately pulled out the details of the guy on her computer.

"Tito Costa, forty-nine, arrested for robbing a bank, currently fugitive for missing his court date. Fairly high bond, but that's because his loot is still missing. One ugly dude."

I went to take a look. "I wonder what's happened to him."

"I'd say he was thrown through a window face-first, and patched up without much care for where each piece belonged."

Jackson emerged from his office, still furious. "And why the hell weren't you answering your phone?"

His angry opening apropos of nothing threw me a little, but I shrugged. "The new one isn't operational yet and I haven't heard the old one ring." I dug into my bag and pulled out both phones. The cardboard box of the new phone was dented in the middle and I winced, fearing the worst. And my old phone was definitely toast, the display sadly crushed.

I opened the box that contained the new phone and pulled it out. To my immense relief, it was intact, the Styrofoam packaging having protected it.

"This one made it."

"Next time, don't try to stand in the way of a running fugitive."

I crossed my arms over my chest, miffed. "I was trying to help."

"You could've hurt yourself! Did you?"

I wasn't going to tell him about my tailbone, thank you very much. Some things weren't done, and inviting my boss to gaze at my ass was one of them, no matter how fine it looked in the tight pants.

Really fine, FYI.

"No." And since I couldn't leave well and truly alone, I continued: "You didn't get the guy, then?"

"No. But don't worry, I will. This is personal now."

When Jackson calmed down, he showed me the basics of skip tracing. He pulled out an incredible amount of information on Tito Costa, including his address and those of his family and associates.

"Let's go check these out," Jackson said. "It's more bounty hunter work than P.I.'s, but the basics are the same."

Costa lived in East New York, the easternmost neighborhood of Brooklyn before Queens. It had a bad reputation, but it looked like a small town, because the houses were low and quite a few of them had false façades like in old Western towns.

Costa had an apartment above a phone repair shop in a two-story building on a stretch of hole-in-the-wall businesses. The entrance was towards the sidewalk, between the phone repair shop and a drycleaner, and it had iron bars on it. The door was locked, which didn't surprise either of us.

"Let's ask here," Jackson said, heading to the dry-cleaner. "Everyone needs clean clothes."

An old woman was sitting on a tall stool behind the service counter. She had graying black hair in a tight bun, a round figure in a formless dress, and a permanent scowl on her wrinkled face. She had trouble under-standing what Jackson wanted to know, and when she spoke, her accent was heavy.

"I know not him," she said when he showed her Costa's photo. "I ask son."

She turned to yell to the backroom in a foreign language—Polish, I'd guess, because I'd heard Mrs. Pasternak use similar language, with a similar tone, I might add, with Olek. A moment later a man emerged. He was only in his early twenties, and I couldn't believe he was the old lady's son and not her grandson. Maybe she was younger than she looked, or she didn't know the correct word.

"That guy? I haven't seen him in ages," he said when Jackson showed him the photo and a ten dollar bill. "I'd remember. Difficult to forget a face like that."

We didn't have any better luck in the phone repair shop, or the other addresses Jackson had, all of them in the same area. But it was a good introduction to what the work entailed: lots of driving around and asking questions from people who didn't want to answer.

It was closing time by the time we returned to the office, and Cheryl was already packing her things for the night. "I didn't expect to see you back today."

"We're fetching a camera for me," I told her, excited. "I get to do a stakeout on my own tonight."

"Great! Where is it?"

"Near my parents' house. It's a nice residential area so I'll be all right on my own." It wasn't so much my concern as it was Jackson's. I leaned over to scratch

Pippin goodbye and a thought occurred to me: "Would you mind terribly letting Pippin come with me tonight?"

She looked disappointed. "Why?"

"Old ladies in the neighborhood tend to become suspicious of people loitering outside their houses. A dog would give me a plausible reason to be there."

"All right," she sighed. "Make sure he doesn't eat anything he shouldn't, and gets plenty of exercise. Otherwise he becomes excitable in the middle of the night." She handed the leash to me and left after one final scratch between Pippin's ears. He stared forlornly after her and I hoped I hadn't bitten off more than I could chew.

Jackson emerged from his office with a small camera and proceeded to show me how it worked. To my relief it wasn't terribly complicated. I took the camera and Pippin and we were off to my parents'.

The subway ride was faster during the evening rush than the car, but not much more comfortable. It was hot and a horrible crush. I had to hold Pippin so he wouldn't be trampled over, which made me even more sweaty and uncomfortable. I wasn't in the best of moods when I reached my parents' house, and matters didn't improve with the surprise that waited for me when I led Pippin in.

Travis.

My parents were gathered in the living room with him and they all turned to face me when we entered, indicating they'd been waiting for me. "Is that a dog?"

Mother asked when she spotted Pippin, who instantly decided she was his new best friend.

"Yes, the one I found."

"I'm allergic to those things," Travis said, coming to give me a hug. "Why did you bring him here?"

"I didn't know you'd be here, did I." Although I should've guessed. He liked to meddle in my life. "I need him as a ruse on my stakeout."

"Trevor is allergic to them too."

"Yeah, but he's not a fuss."

Travis frowned. He was the spitting image of Dad, with the same handsome face and dark Irish coloring. He had put himself through college with a varsity scholarship, and his six-foot frame was still lean and muscled. He was smart enough to get into Harvard Law, which he'd paid for with scholarships and part-time jobs. He could've chosen any field of law, and was courted to high-end businesses, but he chose criminal law and Brooklyn Defender Services instead.

And he was a good defense attorney. He would go to places—political places—which I think was the reason he'd become a public defender. And it wouldn't hurt his chances in the political arena that his father-in-law was the DA for Queens County.

The two of us were polar opposites when it came to ambition and we didn't really understand each other. The age difference didn't help either.

"What's this about becoming a P.I.?" he asked after

Pippin was banished to the back porch when Travis's eyes started to water—I guess he really was allergic—and we had sat to dinner.

"I lost my job and the opportunity was there."

"Couldn't you finally finish college?"

"With what money?"

He frowned. "What about community college?"

"I'd still need a job to pay the rent."

"You could move in with me and Melissa and give up your apartment."

"And become a free nanny to your brats? I don't think so." Travis's four-year-old twins, Brandon and Chad—or, as I liked to call them, Damien 1 and Damien 2—were spawns of hell as far as I was concerned.

"My children aren't brats," Travis said offended. Mom inhaled sharply too. She adored her grandsons.

"Meanwhile, you work late every night, and sometimes on Saturdays too, just to avoid going home."

"That's because we're overworked."

I smiled. "Well, if you're so overworked and you don't like my new job, why don't you offer me a job instead?"

"I didn't say I don't like your new job."

"What's this about, then?"

"Jackson Dean isn't exactly the kind of man I want around my baby sister."

I snorted in surprise. "He used to be here all the time."

"I didn't care back then."

"Well, here and now he's a different person who's made something of himself. If he's good enough to work for the DA's office *and* yours, he's good enough to be my boss."

The good thing about Travis was that he could be won over by a reasonable argument. "Fine. Just be careful."

"Always."

Travis took his leave right after dinner and I got up too to fetch Pippin from the back porch. When we reached the street, Travis was standing by his car, a new and sleek Mercedes he couldn't possibly afford with a civil servant's salary. But his wife was rich and he wasn't above taking advantage of it. He was finishing a smoke, clearly waiting for me.

"Are you sure you'll be all right? I didn't want to say anything with Mom around, but I know the kinds of jobs Jackson gets."

I patted him on the shoulder. His concern was genuine, so I should be grateful. "I'll be fine."

"Do you need anything?"

I hesitated. "Well, I guess I could use a twenty until my last paycheck from the café clears."

What? He offered.

He instantly took out his wallet and gave me a fifty. "Ask for more if you need."

Brothers. You had to love them.

Chapter Nine

Ten minutes later, Pippin and I made our first pass by Mrs. Jenkins' house. I was armed with the camera and a bunch of small plastic bags Mom had said were absolutely necessary when walking a dog.

"You will not leave his droppings behind."

I hadn't quite imagined scooping poop from the sidewalk when I took this job, but I didn't argue. The last thing I needed was the neighborhood watch descending on me while I tried to be unnoticed. I didn't want Mrs. Bradshaw, who was the president of the neighborhood watch, to descend on me even when I wasn't trying to be unnoticed. So I picked diligently after Pippin.

The woman from the previous night hadn't arrived yet—or at least her car wasn't there—so Pippin and I walked to the next crossing, pausing whenever he wanted, and then made our way slowly back again. To slow our progress further, I practiced using the camera by taking tons of photos of Pippin, who posed gracefully when I asked him to. Whoever he belonged to had clearly liked to photograph him a lot.

I'd managed to choose the appointed dog-walking time of the neighborhood, so my presence wasn't marked. I got unexpected help from the other dog-walkers too, because they wanted to stop and chat with me, which gave me perfect opportunities to keep an eye on the house.

When dusk began to fall, we'd spent almost an hour traipsing the same stretch of street. Pippin didn't mind, but I was contemplating calling Dad to bring the car.

I decided to make one more round, but didn't get far when we were stopped again, this time by a man who came down the driveway of a house we were passing. I knew the house; it belonged to the family of the girl Trevor had taken to the senior prom. Suzy Carter. She had consequently broken his heart when she cheated on him with his best friend. Not at the prom though.

I didn't know this man, but that wasn't a wonder. The houses here had changed owners since I'd moved away. He wasn't interested in me anyway, but leaned over to make Pippin's acquaintance. Theme of the evening, but I wasn't offended. It rendered me kind of invisible, which was what I needed.

When he straightened up he positively loomed over me, making me take an involuntary step back. He was in his early thirties, well over six-feet tall, six-three at least, and too muscled for his suit jacket, even though it looked tailor-made. The collar of his dark silk shirt was un-buttoned; his thick black hair was combed backwards;

his black brows were straight, and his dark brown eyes were deep set. I guess I would've considered him handsome if I hadn't been so intimidated by him. He looked like a mafia enforcer, more than anything. Pippin seemed perfectly happy with him, but he liked everyone.

"What's his name?" the man asked. He had a cultured, baritone voice, which threw me a little. I'd expected something harsh.

"Pippin." I was amazed how calm I sounded. As luck would have it, the street had become deserted and I couldn't call anyone to help me if it came to that. He wasn't even threatening me, yet I was extremely nervous.

"Cute name."

"Cute dog," I answered.

"What breed is he?"

"I haven't got a clue."

That earned me a funny look. "You got him from a shelter?"

"He belongs to a friend and I forgot to ask." I hadn't made a conscious decision to lie, it just came out.

"I've been looking for a dog exactly like that," he said. "He ran away from my boss's daughter."

My heart stopped. "I'm sorry to hear that. Was it around here?" I tightened my hold of Pippin's leash.

"No, yours just caught my attention, that's all."

"Do you live here?" I nodded towards the house he'd come from.

He smiled and didn't look quite so intimidating, but I didn't lower my guard. "No, but my girlfriend does." I now detected a slight Jersey accent in his voice.

"Suzy Carter?"

"Yes. Do you know her?"

"She broke my brother's heart."

He grinned. "I'll keep that in mind."

I smiled, relieved that he wasn't about to attack me. "Well, I hope you find your boss's dog."

"Thanks."

Suzy emerged from the house just then, looking much like she had back in high school, small and curvy, in tight clothes and with a lot of wavy red hair. She was dwarfed by her boyfriend when she reached us, even in her mile high heels. Then again, I was dwarfed by him, and I was three inches taller than her. I was momentarily distracted as I wondered about the bedroom logistics between the two.

"Tracy? Tracy Hayes? I haven't seen you in a dog's age. What are you doing here? Did you move back home? I hear Trevor still lives with your parents. Couldn't find a job?"

She'd fired the questions with an annoying nasal voice so fast I couldn't get an answer in. So I answered them all at once. "Walking a dog, no, yes, he has a job—he's a homicide detective."

She wasn't impressed. "He can't exactly afford this, then." She made a sweeping gesture to a large black

BMW SUV parked by the curb. The big man got into the driver's seat with a friendly wave—he probably wouldn't fit in a smaller car—and she took the passenger's seat with a sneer. I found myself wishing the guy would dump her sorry ass, and I didn't even know him.

They drove away and Pippin and I continued down the street, but I couldn't shake the sense of unease the encounter had caused. For all I knew, Pippin was the dog the man had been looking for, yet the decision to lie had been instinctive. I should've asked for details, but I simply hadn't been able to make myself to.

Perhaps Jackson's notion that people were strange had echoed in the back of my mind. Maybe the man had been sincere—why would he have lied about his boss's daughter's dog—but he might just as well have wanted a cute dog for Suzy.

Definitely a good reason to lie.

Then I snorted a laugh. Only a day in this job and I was already paranoid.

I got a new topic to think about when the car from the previous night pulled over outside Mrs. Jenkins' house. I was too far from the house and dusk had come, but it was definitely the same woman who exited the car. I recognized the confident gait when she made her way to the front door in her high heels.

It was too dark to take photos, but I clicked the camera a couple of times anyway, and then the woman was already inside the house. I checked the images, but they were black. Disappointed, I pondered my options. I should probably leave, but Jackson had told me the husband would come home tomorrow and he expected results. I wasn't allowed to take photos through the windows, so I had to think of something else.

I needed a direct approach. I had to get inside the house.

I devised a cunning plan.

I hid the plastic bags Mom had given me under a shrub and crossed the street. I paused by a little bush in front of the red house, let Pippin sniff around it, and then made a show of looking for a poop bag from my pockets—as if anyone was watching, or able to see anything in the dark. Unsuccessful—duh—I assumed a look of acute embarrassment and went to the door.

I had to knock twice before the door was opened by a woman a few years older than me. She was about my height, had nice, strong Mediterranean features, and her long black hair fell down her back in heavy waves. She was wearing a red satin robe that showcased her curvy figure perfectly. I'd kill for cleavage like hers.

Definitely a woman having an affair.

"Yes?" She wasn't happy for being interrupted, but I didn't let that deter me.

"I'm really sorry, but my dog did his business right on your driveway and I'm all out of plastic bags. I don't know what happened. Maybe they've dropped from my pocket, because I could swear I took plenty. Anyway, I was wondering if you had something I could remove it with?" I gave her a hopeful and apologetic smile. She peered over my shoulder towards the alleged scene of the crime, but of course couldn't see anything in the dark.

"Don't sweat it, I'll remove it myself." She went to close the door but Pippin had snuck in, which gave me an excuse to stop her while I ineffectively tugged the dog's leash.

"Oh, I couldn't possibly let you do that. What would the neighbors say? A little plastic bag will do, an old bread bag or something?"

She sighed and retreated, allowing me into the hallway. "Don't let the dog come in any further," she said, heading to the kitchen.

The moment she disappeared from sight, I peeked into the living room, which was set for a romantic encounter, with candles and red wine on the coffee table. Then someone started down the stairs and I retreated, picking up the dog, as if I'd been retrieving him all along.

First I saw a pair of long, shapely legs I could only dream of having, then a short black silk negligee, as the woman was wearing nothing else. I'd say Mrs. Jenkins was absolutely having an affair. Then the woman's face came into view, and we both startled when we recognized one another.

"You!"

My sister Tessa and I stared at each other, both utterly shocked.

Chapter Ten

"WHAT THE HELL ARE YOU doing here?" Tessa demanded, descending the last steps to the hall.

She was thirty-three and looked every bit as amazing as when she'd put herself through med-school by modeling. She had Dad's height and looks, which were as good on a woman as they were on a man, especially with the short pixie cut she favored. I'd always felt like an ugly duckling next to her, and dying my hair auburn only emphasized our differences.

"I could definitely ask the same."

"I asked first." She might have the supermodel looks, but she'd always had the no-nonsense attitude of a doctor, even when we were kids. She expected to be answered. I wanted to sulk. This was not how my plan was supposed to go.

"I was walking the dog and ran out of poop bags," I said, lifting Pippin towards her just as Mrs. Jenkins came from the kitchen with a plastic bag in her hand. She paused when she saw us.

"What's going on?"

"My parents sent my little sister to spy on us."

"They did no such thing. They have absolutely no idea." I'd had no idea Tessa was into women, and our parents wouldn't even be able to imagine it.

"What's with the dog ruse, then?"

"It's not a ruse," I said, indignant.

"You don't own a dog."

"He's not my dog. I found him and I'm taking care of him until I find the owner."

"It's Richard, isn't it?" Mrs. Jenkins said, leaning heavily against the hallway wall. "He's found out about us."

Guilt stabbed in my gut that I couldn't keep from my face, and Tessa was onto me instantly. "Out with it!" She looked angry—and a little frightened too. I couldn't remember ever seeing my sister frightened.

My heart fell. This was supposed to be an easy gig. All I had to do was to get the evidence of Mrs. Jenkins' infidelity. I didn't have to care for the whys and whos of it. But this was my sister. I couldn't sell her out and perhaps ruin her chance for happiness in the process.

I'd have to tell everything to Tessa and take my chances with Jackson later. I'd lose my job before I'd even properly begun. That had to be a new record.

I sighed. "I work for a private detective. Mr. Jenkins hired us to find out if his wife was having affairs while he was out of town."

"Affairs? Plural?" Mrs. Jenkins was outraged.

"Work for a P.I.? Since when?" Tessa demanded, claiming my attention.

"Since yesterday. Probably not after this."

"Serves you right for skulking in the bushes."

"I wasn't skulking."

"What are you going to tell him?" Mrs. Jenkins asked what worried her more. I could sympathize, but not much. I was a jilted woman myself.

"Can't you tell your husband? It has to be better than finding out from a P.I."

"Can't you just keep quiet?" Tessa retorted.

"That's okay," Mrs. Jenkins sighed. I really should ask her first name, but this didn't seem like a good time to inquire. "I can't go on like this any longer."

"Are you sure?" Tessa asked, wrapping an arm around Mrs. Jenkins' shoulders. She sounded more solicitous that I'd ever heard before. She usually had the curt manners of a surgeon.

"Yes. I just wish I could hurt him the way he hurt me."

I didn't know the details of that, but I knew one thing: "Nothing hurts like seeing the evidence of your spouse's infidelity with your own eyes."

"But if he has evidence that I've been unfaithful, he'll get everything."

"What do you need from him that I can't give you?" Tessa asked her. They exchanged a long, intimate look that made me uncomfortable, as if I were trespassing on a private moment. Then Mrs. Jenkins nodded.

"Let's do it," she said resolutely.

Tessa smiled and kissed her. Then she turned to me. "Do you have a camera?"

"Yes."

"Go outside and take a photo of the two of us on the couch," she ordered me.

"I'm not allowed to take photos through windows without the consent of the people being photographed," I said primly.

Tessa rolled her eyes. "We're giving you our consent, aren't we?" I turned to Mrs. Jenkins, who hesitated but then nodded.

"I'm Tracy Hayes, by the way." I offered her my hand and she shook it with a startled smile.

"Angela Jenkins. I'm not usually this irresolute. It's just that finding out Richard knows shook me a little."

When I got to the porch, Tessa and Angela were already on the couch, busily making out. I tried to ignore that it was my sister there, kissing a woman, and just fired the camera away. They'd placed themselves so that Angela's face was in clear view, whereas you couldn't recognize Tessa. But Tessa's boob was coming out of her negligee, so you had no doubt it was another woman there.

Poor Mr. Jenkins would get the shock of his lifetime.

I returned indoors to fetch Pippin I'd left in the hallway, and had to clear my throat a couple of times to get their attention. "I'm going now."

Tessa sent me away with a wave of her hand. "Don't tell Mom and Dad," she shouted just before the door closed behind us.

As we reached the sidewalk, Pippin stopped to do his business by the bush, forcing me to use the plastic bag I'd taken from Angela after all. I felt curiously vindicated.

A bag of poop in one hand, leash in the other, I returned to my parents', humming a tune as I went. Not bad for the first assignment.

Trevor pulled over just as I was about to enter the house.

"Long day," I said to him when he reached the porch.

"You too, I see." He leaned over to scratch Pippin's ears. "I'm allergic to dogs, you know."

"I know. Travis reminded me today."

"He was here?"

"Was he ever."

He winced in sympathy. We made our way to the kitchen to have leftovers for supper—with Pippin. Trevor wasn't a fuss.

"I thought I made it clear to Dad that Jackson's a good guy."

"Travis remembered him from their childhood."

"Headed to the juvie?" he asked as he put the food into the microwave.

"According to Jackson himself, yes." I gave Pippin some water and then set the table.

"He turned himself around though."

"That's what I told Travis."

He nodded and we sat down to eat by the kitchen table. "And how did your stakeout go?"

"Really well." I couldn't help the smile spreading on my face.

"Okay, out with it. Was Mrs. Jenkins having an affair?"

"She was indeed."

"Did you get pictures?"

"Like you wouldn't believe." I meant it literally.

"Can I see them?"

I wasn't about to deny my brother the pleasure of seeing his big sister make out with a woman. "Absolutely." I fished the camera out of my bag and showed him the photos.

"That's ... a woman." He sounded both stunned and appalled.

"Like it's the worst you've seen in your life," I said, snorting.

"No, I mean I didn't expect this."

"That's not even the best part." I couldn't keep my mirth in. "Do you recognize the other woman?"

"Is she supposed to be one of my exes?" He studied the pictures more closely on the tiny camera screen. "I'm sure I'd recognize a breast that fine if I'd had the pleasure. So who is she?"

I'd only promised not to tell Mom and Dad. I glanced around to see they weren't in earshot. "Tessa."

He pulled back so fast he hit his head on the kitchen window. “The fuck she is. Isn’t she with that guy, what’s his name, Paul?”

“Not anymore I’d say. And good riddance.” I’d never liked the sleazy bastard.

“You’re sure it’s her? How can you tell from that?”

I told him the whole story. By the time I finished, he was bellowing in laughter. “Only you could botch a simple surveillance job.”

“I didn’t botch it. I got the evidence, didn’t I.” But he just kept laughing.

“Poor Jackson doesn’t know what he bargained for with you.”

“Bah.” I crossed my arms, sulking.

Trevor gave Pippin and me a lift home and I asked him to let us out outside a convenience store a little down the street from my building. “I need to buy dog food.”

It wasn’t terribly late and I didn’t expect trouble, so I sent Trevor away when he would’ve waited. But when I exited the store, I got a funny feeling that I was being watched.

I looked surreptitiously around as I let Pippin sniff the fire hydrant for interesting smells. I didn’t see anything or anyone, but I hurried the dog in, feeling safe only after I’d locked my door and put the safety chain on. And when Pippin woke me up in the middle of the night, indicating he wanted to go out, I ignored him and continued to sleep. I would not go back out, not even for a dog.

I paid for it in the morning, when the first thing I stepped on when I got out of bed was a puddle of dog wee.

Chapter Eleven

IN THE LIGHT OF DAY MY PREVIOUS night's fears seemed silly. No one was watching me and no one followed us when Pippin and I headed to the subway. I had plenty of chances to check, because Pippin wanted to leave his mark on every bush between my home and the station.

Or maybe he was protesting of his treatment the previous night. He certainly gave that impression when he saw Cheryl at the office, rushing to her like she was his savior.

Really. Miss one walk and that's what I get?

I was anxious though, when I settled on the couch in Jackson's office with a large mug of coffee. This was the moment of truth.

"How did it go yesterday?" Jackson started without preambles.

"I got the evidence, but I'm not sure you'll like what happened," I said.

"And what happened?" He directed his best cop gaze at me and I confessed everything like a child caught with her hand in a cookie jar. He blinked when I finished. Then he started laughing.

"That's so incredible no one will believe it."

That didn't help my anxiety. "As long as Mr. Jenkins will."

"Let's see the photos, then." He uploaded them to his computer and opened the first one. His eyebrows shot up. "Wow."

"I know."

"These are really good photos." He leaned closer and I was pretty sure he was checking Tessa's assets and not the photographic quality. I tried not to feel miffed.

"These should convince Mr. Jenkins." He shook his head ruefully. "I used to have such a crush on Tessa at school, but she wouldn't give me the time of day. Knowing she's into women makes it sting a little less."

I didn't know if Tessa had been gay already at school—she'd definitely been well closeted if she had—but I nodded.

"So I did good?"

He smiled. "You did good." I smiled back, relieved.

We worked in the office the whole morning. Jackson had paperwork to do and I had to study, but he had time to show me some secrets of the trade too. Before I knew it, it was time for lunch. Since Pippin needed his walk, Cheryl headed out to fetch us something to eat. I could've used a walk too—I wasn't accustomed to sitting down all day—but I didn't protest. The novelty of non-achy feet hadn't worn off yet.

The door to the reception area was open, so when two men walked in soon after Cheryl had left, we saw them immediately. The first of them was in his early fifties. He was wearing a light gray summer suit and a pink silk shirt, and had lifted his shades over sleekly combed black hair. He looked perfectly normal and respectable, but I was instantly on guard. Maybe it was the way he cased the reception room before proceeding to Jackson's office and giving the doorframe a polite knock. Maybe it was my waitress's intuition that allowed me to spot the customers most likely to cause trouble with their order.

Maybe it was the huge man who followed him in. The same man who had shown interest in Pippin the previous evening, still tall and muscled in his fine suit. Still intimidating.

I froze on my seat.

"Jackson Dean?" the first man asked. My boss got up to shake his hand. "Craig Douglas."

The other man wasn't introduced and he remained standing by the door like a bodyguard. I kept glancing at him, but he didn't indicate in any way that we had already met, his face calm and impassive—and somehow more threatening for it. I guess that was his purpose.

Jackson showed Mr. Douglas to the guest chair, taking a seat behind his desk. "What can I do for you?"

"I saw your poster. The one for a dog you've found. I believe he's mine."

The presence of the big man had made me anticipate it, but I was still disappointed. I couldn't believe Pippin would belong to him. He was such a happy dog, whereas Mr. Douglas—and definitely his goon—looked like he belonged to the mafia. I didn't trust him, and I was instantly sure he was lying.

Not so Jackson. "Excellent."

My heart sank. He wasn't going to give Pippin to these guys, was he? I wanted to protest, but kept my mouth shut.

"If I could get the description so we'll know it's the right dog. And then there's the matter of a finder's fee, of course."

"I'm willing to pay five hundred dollars if he's my dog," Mr. Douglas said. He sounded sincere, but I almost huffed in disbelief. No one paid that much for a missing dog. He pulled an expensive cell phone out of the inner pocket of his jacket, and flicked through the photos for the one he wanted.

"Is this the dog?" He handed the phone over the desk to Jackson, who took a look at the photo and frowned.

"I'm not sure. I didn't find him myself. We're helping a client. What do you think, Tracy?"

I could breathe more easily. Jackson knew perfectly well what Pippin looked like. And there was no client, which had to mean that he didn't trust the men either.

I went to take a look too, my legs shaking only a little. To my disappointment, the photo was definitely of Pippin. He was posing perfectly like yesterday. I tried to control my expression, but my face simply wouldn't cooperate.

Mr. Douglas leaned towards us, eager. "It's him, isn't it?"

"I'd say so, yes," I said carefully. "What's his name?"

Was it my imagination or did the man hesitate a heartbeat?

"Buster."

I lifted my brows in surprise. "That's a mouthful for such a small dog."

"My son named him."

It was a perfectly good explanation—and one that I didn't buy for a second, and not least because the goon had talked about his boss's daughter's dog. But I'd got my face back in control. I gave him my best smile I used when I was lying to customers, like, 'Yes, that fish was caught today'. It had been a particularly trying restaurant to work for.

"Well, I'm happy to tell you that we've found your Buster."

Mr. Douglas smiled, relieved. "Wonderful. When can I get him?"

"Tomorrow." This time I didn't even blink when I told the lie. "We placed him into foster care, and we can have them bring him here in the morning. Say ten o'clock?"

Mr. Douglas's good mood vanished. "I'm not sure that suits me at all. Maybe you could give me the address. I'll fetch him myself."

I sharpened my best smile, courtesy of years of handling difficult customers, and looked him straight in the eye. "Surely you understand that the people taking care of him have strict orders to give him only to us. They're good people. You've nothing to worry about even if you wait one more day."

I prepared to argue, but Jackson got up, and to my relief Mr. Douglas did too, after only a short hesitation.

"I'm happy we found the rightful owner," Jackson said with a reassuring smile. "Buster will be glad to return to you in the morning."

He rounded the desk and calmly shook Mr. Douglas's hand. Then he directed the men out. As the goon exited, he glanced back and winked at me. Winked! So he had recognized me after all.

Jackson was grinning when he returned to his desk. "Buster my ass. This case just turned interesting."

"You've no idea. I saw the goon yesterday and he was interested in Pippin."

Jackson stilled. "How did he find you?"

"Pure coincidence. His girlfriend lives across the street from the Jenkins'. But he may have followed me to my home." I shivered, remembering the sensation of being watched the previous evening. "And maybe even here in the morning. Though I could swear no one was following me." The big guy wasn't exactly easy to miss, and neither was his car.

Jackson looked grim. "He must have followed you. And then maybe came across the poster when he reached this neighborhood. But they're willing to take the public route, so that's good."

I didn't want to think of what the private route might have been.

"What do you think this is about?"

"Nothing legal, that's for sure. Mr. Douglas was a tad too eager. Maybe Pippin was stolen for ransom, and then Douglas lost him for some reason. Whatever it is, money has to be really good for him to go through this much trouble to get him back."

"Oh, poor Pippin. So how do we find the right owner?"

"I'll check the police reports. But I wouldn't get my hopes up. He could be stolen from anywhere. And I'll definitely upload the photos of those two to a facial recognition program."

"You got their photos?"

He patted a small camera perched on top of his computer monitor. "What do you think this is here for?" I hadn't given it a thought, but now I realized it was facing the clients and not him, like it would if it were meant for video conferences.

He picked up his phone and called Cheryl and told her not to return to the office and to keep Pippin safe. There was an excited gleam in his eyes when he finished.

"There's nothing more we can do until the facial recognition is finished. Let's head out for lunch, since we won't be having it delivered after all. And then we'll go find Costa. I have a good feeling about it."

Chapter Twelve

INSTEAD OF A QUICK BITE IN one of the many eateries within walking distance of the agency, we got into Jackson's car. He chose directions apparently at random, going a couple of blocks one way and five blocks another and then turning again.

"Do you think we're being followed?" I asked when I finally figured out what he was doing.

"Better safe than sorry."

I only recognized where we were when he drove to Kensington, past the house where Suzy Collins lived. There wasn't a black BMW outside it, but I hadn't expected there to be. However, in the Jenkins' driveway there was a sporty Audi.

"I take it Mr. Jenkins is home," I noted.

"He'll be coming over tomorrow, so we'll have until then to figure out how to break the news to him." He looked like he wasn't looking forward to it either.

He drove to 18th Avenue, which denoted the southern end of Kensington, and pulled over in front of an Irish slash sports bar. As close to my parents' as it was, I'd never been there, but that wasn't a surprise. I'd seldom had a chance to eat out when I was a waitress.

It was a hole-in-the-wall eatery, long and fairly narrow, with cozy booths on the left and a long gleaming mahogany bar on the right, and even a small stage at the back. Sports were on the TV's hanging from the ceiling, and the portions were large enough to please truck drivers. At lunch time, though, the clientele looked to be cops from the 70th Precinct that was only two blocks from the bar. And since it was where Trevor worked, I wasn't surprised to find him there.

He was sharing a booth with Detective Blair Kelley, his partner since he'd started in homicide. She was in her early forties and the senior in their partnership, a tall and rather formidable looking woman with a dark skin and short-cropped hair. Her severe manners were a stark opposite to my fairly easygoing brother, but they had always got along well. I'd met her a couple of times and liked her. Jackson knew her of old too, so no introductions were needed when we took seats in their booth.

"I'm glad I ran into you," I said to Trevor after we'd received our food—fairly good but pretty greasy. "Have you kept any contact with Suzy Collins?"

He put a hand dramatically to his heart as if I'd stabbed him. "How can you mention her name?"

Since six years hadn't eased the pain of my husband's betrayal, I wasn't entirely sure he was funning, but I pressed on. "The reason I ask is that I want to know more about the guy she's currently dating."

That caught his interest, so I told him what had happened earlier and that I'd met the guy the previous evening. He frowned when I was finished.

"Why didn't you tell me about the man yesterday?"

"I didn't remember him. The events that followed kind of wiped him out of my mind."

He shook his head as a smile spread on his face. "You heard?" he asked Jackson.

"Yes. I'm heartbroken." He wiped an imaginary tear from his cheek.

Detective Kelley cocked a questioning brow at me, so I told her about the great revelation. She would hear it eventually anyway, as partners tended to share things. "No one was heartbroken when I came out," she said, amused. She had a nice, low voice that held a hint of command even in a casual conversation.

"That's because no one was surprised," my brother said rather unhandsomely, but his partner just rolled her eyes. He returned to our original topic. "You're saying Suzy might be dating a what, dog-napper?"

I shrugged. "Possibly. Or maybe he's in a more lucrative field of crime. The man drove a BMW X6." It wasn't exactly a cheap car. "And his accent was Jersey, as was Douglas's."

Trevor nodded. "It wouldn't surprise me if she was dating a mafia goon. Her first husband is serving time for drugs. He worked for that MacRath guy." That caught Jackson's interest too. "I'll ask around. But you'll owe me. It's my ex we're talking about."

"I understand. I wouldn't go near my ex even for you."

He looked amused. "Oh? Then why are you here?"

"What do you mean? Jackson brought us." I gave my boss a questioning glance, but he shook his head, not knowing what Trevor was talking about either.

"Take a look there." Trevor nodded behind me towards the other end of the long mahogany bar and I turned around to look. At first I didn't understand what he meant. There were a couple of uniforms standing in front of the bar, chatting with the guy behind it, but I didn't know either of them. Then the bartender threw his head back and laughed, a raspy, joyous sound that I instantly recognized. My entire body froze.

Scott Brady, my scumbag of an ex-husband.

Seeing him for the first time since our divorce was a shock to my system I was utterly unprepared for. I wanted to flee, or hide, but since my body couldn't decide which, I remained petrified on the spot. "Couldn't you warn me?" I hissed at Trevor.

"I thought you knew," he said, but he had the good grace to look apologetic.

"How the hell should I know? I haven't paid any attention to him in years." That wasn't entirely true. I'd followed the success of his band, but it had broken up two years after we divorced, after which I'd lost track of him. He hadn't tried to contact me either.

Then I smiled, satisfied. "At least he's working in a bar too."

My companions cleared their throats and glanced at each other. Jackson was the one who spoke. "Actually, he owns the bar."

Fury surged through me, instant and irrational. "We're leaving." I shot up and marched out, not looking back. I was waiting by the car before Jackson reached it. He had the good sense to not speak. He started the engine and we headed east.

I fumed the entire ride. How dare Scott be more successful than me? Ex-spouses should be miserable after the divorce. But it had been me who had slaved in minimum wage jobs for years, trying to make ends meet.

Not that it was much different from when we'd been married. What little the band had made had gone to keeping the tour going, accommodations in cheap motels, gas, food and car repair. When we divorced, Travis had been determined to get me my fair share of what I'd put in to the band's success with my unpaid work, but since Scott had owned practically nothing, all I'd got was his car. I'd paid the deposit for my apartment with what little it fetched me.

We were already in Brownsville before I calmed down and was able to concentrate on the matter at hand. It was a neighborhood that consisted mostly of public housing developments. People there were poor and—quite frankly—hopeless. It used to be the crime capital of New York, and the crime rates kept high there despite declining elsewhere in Brooklyn.

"These kinds of neighborhoods are the reason I'd have preferred a sturdy guy for my apprentice instead of you," Jackson said to me as he drove to our destination. I could only nod in answer. The place didn't make me feel safe. Young men were loitering in street corners, their eyes keen as they watched us pass.

However, when we finally pulled over, it was outside a neat redbrick school with a recently refurbished kid-sized yard for track and field, on a street where cars were much like Jackson's, only newer. Low, redbrick apartment buildings lined the street on both sides, and the couple of hole-in-the-wall businesses there were looked fairly well maintained. Not scary at all.

We were here to see Costa's wife. "She should be the least likely person to keep him hidden," Jackson noted when we entered her building.

It was a good assumption—I'd definitely rat my ex out, especially after the revelation I'd just had—but I knew women.

"Do they have children?"

"Two."

"So who'll pay the alimony if he's behind bars?"

Jackson gave me a long stare. "Fuck."

I grinned. "Let's hope I'm wrong, then."

Jackson knocked on the door of Mrs. Costa's apartment, twice, before it opened, and then only as far as the safety chain allowed. A Hispanic woman in her late forties peeked out through the narrow gap and gave us a suspicious look. We couldn't see into the apartment, but we heard two male voices murmuring in the background.

"Yes?"

"Mrs. Costa? I'm Jackson Dean, a private investigator. I'm looking for your husband."

The voices in the apartment cut.

"He's not here."

"He's failed to appear in court. Where might we find him so he can reschedule?"

"How should I know? But wherever he is, he'd better be getting me my money."

"Alimony payment?" Jackson glanced at me from the corner of his eye.

She gave a derisive snort. "He hasn't paid a penny in alimony. No, he's hidden the stash from his latest robbery. He'd better stay free until he's paid me what he owes."

"But you don't know where he's hidden it?"

"If I did, I'd be there myself."

"Well, here's my card in case he fails to find the money and you want to give us a call," Jackson said, digging out a business card from the pocket of his jacket. I was instantly envious of it. I wanted my own business cards too. Mrs. Costa took the card and then slammed the door in our faces without a word.

"That went well."

Chapter Thirteen

"I TAKE IT WE'RE GOING to keep an eye on her apartment?" I said to Jackson when we were back at the car.

"So you heard the voices too?" When I nodded, he smiled. "Good. Always keep an eye and ear on details like that."

"Couldn't we just have gone in and checked?"

"Only if we had the visual of him. Without it we only have the right to enter the home of the fugitive, not other people, unless we have a warrant. Which you would know if you'd read the material I gave you." He shot me a meaningful look and I tried to look chastised.

"Mrs. Costa must've known it," I noted. "She stood so carefully blocking our view."

"Could be."

We settled down to wait, mostly in silence. Jackson retreated into his zone, and without anything more important to distract me, I continued my seething.

I had a lot to seethe about, like how dare Scott look better than when we were married. He was seven years older than me, he should show it. But men only improved as they aged, didn't they. Scott was more built now—he'd had lean, ropey muscles before—and his face had acquired rugged character, which was only emphasized by stubble on his cheeks and his mop of dark blond hair. He'd had long hair when we were married. I tried to find satisfaction in the fact that he wasn't a successful rock star, but even that didn't help.

"You don't have an ex-wife, do you, or you'd show more sympathy," I huffed when I couldn't keep it in anymore. "Or you have one, but you parted as 'friends'." The disdainful quotes were clear in my tone. "Maybe you even see each other from time to time for a cup of coffee." But Jackson only smiled, which aggravated me more. "And how dare Trevor keep this a secret from me?"

Come to think of it, that probably infuriated me the most.

"He didn't have a reason to believe you'd ever end up in that bar."

"That's not the point. He had news about my ex. He should've shared."

I wallowed in my misery and anger until a more pressing topic began to occupy my mind. "What if I need to use the bathroom?"

I probably shouldn't have had that ice tea with lunch, or I should've at least used the restroom before leaving the bar. But that hadn't been an option, had it.

And whose fault was that? Scott's.

Jackson shrugged. "You suffer." Then a slow smile spread on his face. "Unless you're a guy. We can use empty bottles and cups."

Great.

An excruciatingly long half hour later I had to admit defeat. "I need to go." I was out of the car before he could say anything. I quick-marched to the only place nearby that I judged would have a toilet for customers, a hair salon.

"Can I please, please, please use your toilet?" I jumped on the balls of my feet to indicate the urgency.

The hairdresser, a large Jamaican woman in a colorful tie-dyed shirt and cornrows that reached to her buttocks, gave me a long look.

"The toilet is for customers only. Are you a customer?" She had a heavy Jamaican accent too.

"I could be." I looked around. The posters on the walls showed elaborate styles for African hair that my thin hair simply wouldn't turn to. "I might look good in cornrows," I said hesitantly. "But I don't really have time for them now."

"Perhaps you could buy a nice hairclip, then," the woman suggested. She indicated a rack where all sorts of accessories were hanging.

"Yes, I would like one of those. But can I use the bathroom first?"

"Buy first."

My decision-making skills were at zero, all my brain-power focused on more pressing matters in my lower abdomen, but I went to the rack and scanned the wares as fast as I could.

"I'd like that butterfly hairclip," I said, pointing at random to a clip that had a large colorful butterfly made of chiffon and wire on it.

"Excellent choice. Let me get it for you."

I swear glaciers moved faster than her. I was almost crying before she had taken the hairclip down. "That'll be five dollars."

"That's a bit excessive for a hairclip."

"Do you want to haggle or do you want to use the toilet?"

I saw the wisdom of her question and dug out a bill from my pocket. "Here you go."

"Thank you. Now perhaps you'll allow me to adjust it to its place?"

"Okay, but hurry."

But of course she wouldn't hurry. With deliberate movements, she lifted my bangs and secured them on my right temple with the hairclip. "There. The toilet is that way," she drawled. She nodded towards the back, causing the beads in her cornrows to click.

I barely smiled in thanks as I rushed to my appointment. Much relieved, I emerged a little later. "Thank you. You're a life-saver."

"Am I now," she quizzed me with a smile. "Welcome back," she said as her parting words. I exited the salon and strode towards where I'd left Jackson.

He wasn't there.

I turned around, baffled. Then I turned again, more slowly this time, but the street remained empty of a steel gray Toyota Camry and a dark-haired private detective. Just in case though, I made one more turn.

Nothing.

I'd been gone for longer than I'd anticipated—at the time it had felt like eons—but actually less than ten minutes. Surely he could have waited?

Of course he could. So something must have happened.

My stomach plunged in worry. My hands shaking a little, I dug out my new phone from my messenger bag—it was at the bottom—typical—and called him. He had the speaker on and I could hear the noise of the car engine in the background.

"I'm following Costa. He came out and took off in a car. I couldn't wait for you. Go back to the office. I'll meet you there." He sounded purposeful and not at all like he was sorry for abandoning me, but since I probably would've done the same to him, I shrugged it off.

However, that left me with the daunting task of navigating the neighborhood alone—and on foot too. I had no idea where the nearest subway station was, or where the busses here would go. I was as good as lost.

Sighing, I returned to the hair salon.

Five minutes later, the reluctant owner of another overpriced hairclip, I was on my way to the nearest station. It turned out to be five blocks to the north through the less scary part of Brownsville, and no one gave me any trouble.

Relatively short though the walk was, the day was too hot for it, and I was parched by the time I reached the station. So I took a moment to sit down in a café nearby and enjoyed a cold drink. I even had a muffin.

What? I was hungry. My lunch had been interrupted.

That brought Scott back to my mind, but I felt too good to let him trouble me for long. I could get used to this setting my own schedule thing. Besides, I looked kind of nice with the colorful butterflies on my temple, so I had that going for me too.

The subway train car was fairly empty when I hopped in and I got a seat. In the time-honored fashion of commute travelling, I kept my eyes at my feet or on the adverts, and not on people around me. But when the passengers milled in and out at the next station I glanced up—and saw Costa enter the car.

I froze in baffled indecision. Hadn't Jackson said he was following him? Was he mistaken, or had Costa managed to give him the slip? Had Costa hurt Jackson to escape?

My gut clenched at the last thought.

Costa didn't look my way. He likely wouldn't have

recognized me even if he had—our encounter had been brief—but I busied myself with digging out my phone from my bag, keeping my head low. Since there was no reception, I couldn't call my boss to ask if he was okay, so I sent him a text. He would get it as soon as there was a connection again, hopefully at the next station. Until then, I would stay on Costa's tail.

Costa didn't seem to be in a hurry to get off, nor did he look like a man who suspected he was being followed. He sat at the front of the car, not looking at anyone, but his fierce face made sure no one went close to him.

I clutched my phone, ready to send Jackson new information the moment something happened, but nothing did. At least my texts—in plural—seemed to send, so I was hopeful that Jackson knew where we were, and could follow us above ground.

When Costa finally got off the train, it was at Bergen Street station, the station I'd been travelling to, the one right outside the agency. The destination really baffled me. Was he turning himself in? But why here, at the 78th Precinct, when there were stations closer to him?

I kept on his tail up the stairs to the street, proud of how casually I managed it without raising his suspicions—not that it was difficult with so many people about. I was so sure he'd head to the police station that when he chose the opposite direction I almost didn't follow. He wasn't going far, however. I had to blink a few times to understand where he'd gone.

Then I was on the phone to Jackson. "You'd better be close, boss. Because Costa just went into our building."

Chapter Fourteen

"STAY PUT, I'LL BE RIGHT there." Jackson hung up.

I stared at the phone, miffed. Like that was going to happen. This was my case too. The ache in my tailbone attested to that.

I observed through the glass door how Costa got into the elevator, then I rushed in to check its display. Second floor. He was definitely headed to our agency.

My insides flipped in worry, but I didn't let that stop me. I rushed to the stairs and ran up them two at the time. I'd overestimated my fitness and I had to pause on the second floor landing to recover, so that I wouldn't give my approaching away with my loud breathing. I really had thought I was in better shape.

There was no sign of Costa when I entered the second floor hallway, so I pit-patted to the door of the agency. It was wide open and I paused outside. Had he broken in, or had Cheryl returned? But her desk was empty, as was Jackson's desk I could see from the door, but I'd have to get closer to see the rest of his office. Cautiously, I stepped in.

I saw movement in my peripheral vision, but before I could so much as shriek, a hand grabbed hold of my upper arm, and I was yanked to face the badly-sewn-up mug of Tito Costa.

"You're not Jackson Dean." Disgusted, he pushed me away, making me fall on my back for the second time in two days. My new job was really taking a toll on my poor tailbone. "You tell him he leaves my wife alone." He was out of the door before I had time to be scared.

I scrambled up and rushed after him, but the hallway was already empty, so he must have taken the stairs. For a large man, he could move really fast. I reached the elevator just as its doors opened and Jackson stepped out. I skidded to a halt, almost crashing into him. He took a hold of my shoulders.

"Are you all right?"

"Yes, yes. Costa went down the stairs. Hurry."

He didn't ask questions and disappeared into the stairwell too. I contemplated running after them, but my feet decided that they'd had enough excitement for one day and I sank on the floor.

Jackson found me lying there not long after. He wasn't terribly out of breath, so either he was in better shape than I was—duh—or he'd lost Costa again. He paused by my feet, staring down at me with his brows raised, forcing me to speak first.

"You didn't catch him?"

"No, he'd already vanished. Can you get up?"

"I'm considering it."

He smiled. "What's with the butterflies?"

"I'm trying a new style."

"Cute. Gives you real street cred." He leaned over and pulled me to my feet. "Costa didn't hurt you?"

I dusted my clothes and adjusted the butterflies. "Unless you consider being bowled over again. He only wanted to deliver a message to you."

"Which was?"

"Leave his wife alone."

A satisfied smile spread on his face. "We're getting to him."

I followed at his heels to the agency. At the door he paused so abruptly that I banged my face in his back. "Did you open this?"

"How could I?" I retorted, rubbing my nose. "I don't have the key and I don't know the alarm code."

He turned to study the alarm. It had been yanked off the wall, the wires cut. "You don't need code for that." He turned to study the door, which I now realized had splintered around the lock. "Really subtle."

He strode to his office and tapped the computer keyboard on his desk. "This takes pictures once every minute when I'm not here. Let's see what he was about." He watched the feed for a moment and then whistled. "I did not see this option."

I went to take a look and had to agree with him. The photos weren't of Costa. They showed Craig Douglas's goon stand by the open the door—it was intact, so he must have picked the lock—disable the alarm with a code—Jackson's brow furrowed seeing it—and then meticulously go through all the filing cabinets. Time stamp on the photos indicated that he had come in soon after we had left, so he must have been keeping an eye on the agency.

"I bet he was looking for the name and address of the people who are allegedly fostering Buster," I said.

"You'd win that bet."

When the man left, a photo showed him switch on the alarm again. The door was neatly closed after him. A couple of hours later a photo showed Costa stumble through the reception area after breaking the door with great force, and in the next photo the alarm was off the wall. Jackson frowned when a photo showed Costa grab me. Luckily there wasn't one of me on my back.

"Costa did us a favor. I would never have checked these photos if he hadn't been here."

"Should we call the police?"

Jackson nodded, reluctantly. "I guess we have to, so I can claim the insurance. But I'll never live this down."

"Maybe they'll think you've entered the big leagues with enemies who would do this," I said, but he rolled his eyes.

"High profile dog-nappers? That'll give me street cred."

Two uniformed officers arrived gratifyingly fast. Just

because the precinct was around the corner didn't mean we'd be a priority, but it'd been a slow afternoon for them. They weren't terribly interested in the broken lock and alarm, but they took the details down so Jackson could file the insurance claim.

However, the pictures of the goon electrified them. "We'd better call in the lieutenant."

Lonny Peters showed up ten minutes later. He took one look at the photo of the nameless guy and whistled. "Know who that is?"

"No, I don't know," Jackson said, annoyed. "Face recognition software hasn't come up with a result yet and your uniforms weren't forthcoming."

"He's Jonny Moreira, Craig Douglas's henchman."

"I knew that much myself. I just don't know what makes Craig Douglas a person of interest to the police."

"He's Rob MacRath's brother-in-law. From Jersey. Handles much of the drug traffic there."

Jackson pulled up straighter, clearly impressed. "I had no idea."

"We believe he's taking over the business here too, now that MacRath's facing a life behind bars."

"Then why the hell is he going around stealing dogs?"

"What fucking dogs?" Jackson briefed the detective, who looked bemused. "I guess we'd better find out whose dog it is, then."

"Any ideas?"

"Well, with MacRath's trial coming up, it might be a good idea to start with the DA's office." With that, he was out of the agency, leaving Jackson and me staring at each other, bemused.

"So MacRath is the drug lord whose case you helped with, right?"

Jackson's face set in grim lines as he took a seat behind his desk. "Yeah."

"It seems really weird that his drug lord brother-in-law is stealing dogs."

"I think Lonnie's got it right. Pippin belongs to a judge or someone similar."

"Do you really think a judge would be swayed just because his or her dog was held hostage?"

He shrugged. "I've heard stranger things in my life."

I liked Pippin, so if it came to putting a drug lord away or saving the dog, I might have trouble deciding too.

"A juror might be persuaded by it."

"Except they haven't been selected yet."

"So why was the dog here where I could find him?"

"MacRath lives in Prospect Heights. It's the base of his operations, so his brother-in-law likely kept the dog at his place."

"Must be lucrative being a drug lord." I remembered the BMW Moreira drove too.

"Don't get any funny ideas," Jackson said with a smile. I had a more pressing concern.

"Do you think Douglas knows you're involved in his brother-in-law's case?"

"If he didn't know before, he'll know now. Moreira was very thorough."

"Do you think they'll come after you?"

He shrugged, not really concerned. "It's possible, but not probable."

"Should we contact the DA's office?"

"We'd better, though they already have all the evidence I got for them." He glanced at the watch in his wrist. "It's past closing time there. We'll have to leave it tomorrow. Let's call it a day. You can go home."

I was reluctant to leave. I was used to longer days, and the excitement of the day still had me in its grips. I wanted action. There was nothing at home except empty cupboards and the TV, and anything the TV had to offer would pale in comparison with reality. I now understood Trevor's comment about comic relief.

"Shouldn't we come up with a plan first, just in case Douglas comes asking for Pippin in the morning?"

"He actually might. He doesn't know we know they've broken in here."

"Unless they kept an eye on this place the rest of the afternoon and saw the police come and go. What if they come back tonight?"

"I'll be here the whole night. They'll have to go through me."

"You will? Is that safe?"

He smiled. “Safe enough. I can’t leave the place unguarded until I get someone to fix the door and the alarm. But you can go home.”

So I went. Reluctantly.

I scanned the street outside the agency for Douglas and Moreira, but saw neither of them before I descended the steps to the subway platform. In the train, and while walking home from the station, I kept a constant eye out for suspicious activity. By the time I reached my building I was skittish and paranoid.

In short, I was in the perfect mood for a freak-out when I saw a strange man waiting for me outside my apartment door.

Chapter Fifteen

HEART THUDDING IN MY THROAT, I paused right outside the elevator. The man was young, tall, and lanky. He was wearing a dirty T-shirt and frayed jeans, and his hair was a shaggy mop that hadn't been washed in ages. He had a black, tattered guitar case leaning against his legs, and he smelled so pungently of weed that my eyes started to water.

He didn't strike me as someone working for Douglas, but that didn't mean he wouldn't be. Maybe drugs were a perk when one worked for a drug lord.

Then again, he looked rather mellow as he slouched against the wall. I could take him in a fight.

Maybe.

Gathering up my courage, I rummaged through my bag for the pepper spray—why was everything I needed always at the bottom?—and kept my line clear for Mrs. Pasternak's apartment. I'd seek shelter there if necessary. Then I walked closer and addressed him.

"What are you doing here?" I was proud of how demanding I sounded, almost like Dad. "How did you get past Mr. Chlebek?" The janitor kept an eye on people coming and going; he would have stopped this guy.

He lifted his head and his gaze focused slowly on me. "Hey. Wow. Yeah." It took a while longer for him to get his brain to focus. "I came, like, to check out this room?"

My heart missed a beat. "What room?"

He dug into the pocket of his jeans and pulled out a badly crumpled paper and gave it to me. I unfolded it and stared at it in dismay.

It was my ad for the room.

My hand turned clammy and I was having trouble breathing. I had faced violence today, but this casual invasion of my home base felt infinitely worse.

"How did you know it would be here?" I wasn't so stupid that I'd put my address in the ad.

"I, like, checked the address from the e-mail address?"

"You can do that?" I didn't like the sound of it.

"I can."

"Legally?"

That got him thinking—a slow process. "I don't know."

He didn't exactly look like he was capable of any complicated tasks, so I had to wonder how he'd achieved it.

"Well, I can't rent the room to you."

"Aww, man, don't say that. I need a place to stay."

"And I need someone who's good for the rent and doesn't smoke weed."

Dad had the strictest policy against drugs, and the nose of a bloodhound to enforce it. He had made me change rooms in college when he smelled the pot my roommate had smoked. Luckily for me I'd been clean, or I don't know what would've happened. Not that I was entirely blameless during my college year. Dad just hadn't caught me.

The guy looked baffled, as if I'd asked for the moon. "I only smoke, like, recreationally."

"Yeah, well, my brother arrests people professionally, and he doesn't like drugs."

"That's harsh."

"Besides, I don't like guitar players." Not anymore anyway. One colossally failed marriage to a band leader had cured me of that tendency.

"That's cool. This isn't a guitar." He flicked the clasps of the case open and dirty clothes tumbled out. I tried not to gag at the smell.

"I don't think we'd suit. I want a woman as a roommate." Preferably one who liked cleaning.

"Man, that's, like, sexist. I could sue you."

I gave him a slow look. "No, you couldn't."

"Really?"

I had no idea, but I wasn't about to admit it. "It's best you go, before Mrs. Pasternak sees you." She was a formidable woman and would get rid of him in no time.

"Couldn't I, like, stay the night?"

I knew better than to let him in, but he looked so miserable and hopeful at the same time, like a puppy that expects to be kicked but hopes he won't, that I felt my resolution waver.

"Fine. Just for tonight. But I have conditions and they're non-negotiable. First, I'll confiscate your weed. There'll be no recreational anything under my roof. Second, you'll scrub yourself and your clothes clean the moment you come in, and remain clean. And third, if you're not out the moment I say so, I'll call my brother and have him arrest you."

He mulled over my terms for a moment and then nodded. "I can live with that."

His name was Jarod Fitzpatrick, he told me, as we stuffed all his clothes into my washing machine—a hand-me-down from my aunt, but serviceable—as fast as we could while not breathing. He was twenty-one, which was older than I had thought, and he was a graduate student in computer science at Brooklyn College, which he didn't seem old enough for. Not that he always remembered to attend, as he admitted.

"I, like, know everything already. I get bored."

Turned out, when he sobered enough after a long shower to give a comprehensive account of his life, he was a former child wizard who'd learned computers when he was only a little kid and had kept learning ever since. He could've skipped college, including the graduate degree, and sought full-time employment, but his parents had insisted that he study, because it would teach him discipline. Either they were very mistaken in their notion or this was him disciplined.

He'd ambled into the kitchen after his shower wearing nothing but the towel I'd loaned him wrapped around his hips. He wasn't just lanky, he was skinny, and the towel reached twice around him. He didn't smell anymore, and he had combed his wet hair backwards, revealing a rather delicate face and big brown eyes. He kind of reminded me of Pippin, which instantly warmed me to him.

Not good. I'd have to stay firm.

"About the rent. Your share, should I choose to let you stay, would be nine hundred, plus half of the utilities." It was actually only eight hundred, and water and electricity were included, but I needed to scare him off.

"I'm good for that. I work at Lexton Security during the summer break, and weekends during the term. I monitor and counter the illegal activity on their clients' servers. It pays really well."

I blinked, twice, and I still couldn't wrap my mind around what he'd said. "Then why are you desperate for a place to live and look like you've been sleeping rough?"

He shrugged. "My girlfriend kicked me out and these were the only clothes I managed to take with me. I was kind of bummed out and couldn't work up the energy to find a new place, so I've been sleeping wherever."

"Why didn't you go to a motel or something?"

"Oh, I did. I just didn't have the energy to wash my clothes, you know." Or himself, for that matter. He might be a computer genius, but he seemed utterly clueless about life in general. "I can pay you two months in advance." He looked hopeful.

I wanted to tell him I wouldn't keep him that long, but I really needed the money. "You've managed to keep your job at least. Didn't anyone complain about the smell?"

"Nah, I have my own station in the basement."

"Well, I'm not promising anything permanent until I've made some background checks."

"That's cool. But if I'm good enough for a security firm, I'm sure I'm good enough for you."

I couldn't argue with that. "In that case, would you like some dinner? I have cereal, but no milk, and frozen waffles."

There had been the leftovers I'd taken the other day, but I'd eaten them while he took the shower. My offerings weren't much, but Jarod's eyes lit up like I'd promised him a gourmet meal. He probably hadn't eaten in ages.

"I always eat cereal without milk. I'm lactose intolerant."

After we finished eating—both cereals and waffles for Jarod—I showed him the room, which only had the bed left from Jessica. Before I even had a chance to look for clean sheets for him, he dropped on it.

"Can you wake me up in an hour?" With that, he closed his eyes and dozed off as if I wasn't there.

Bemused, I wandered to the couch in the living room and called Jackson. "Can you check someone for me?" I should probably have called Trevor instead, but I didn't want him to barge in here, which he would do the moment he heard about Jarod.

"Sure, though with the phone you could do it yourself."

"Yes, but I probably wouldn't understand the connections, if he belongs to a crime family."

He was silent for a heartbeat. "Who are we talking about?" I told him about Jarod. "You let a potential member of a crime family into your apartment?"

Put like that, it did sound stupid. "He seems harmless. Besides, I need someone to pay the rent or I'll be homeless."

He sighed. "Do you want me to come and get rid of him?"

"Nah, I'll ask Trevor if it comes to that. For now I'd just like to know if he's at all suitable."

"I'll see what I can do." He called me back twenty minutes later. "He's legit. No connections to crime families that I can find, and definitely not to MacRath."

The relief I felt was disproportional. I reminded myself I wasn't going to keep Jarod, so I shouldn't get attached to him.

But I had a nagging feeling the fight was already lost.

Chapter Sixteen

JAROD WOKE UP WITHOUT assistance from me, dressed in his clean clothes, helped himself to coffee, and slumped on the sofa next to me. He looked like a different person—and definitely smelled better.

"Your background check came clean," I told him, and he looked delighted like I'd complimented him.

"Yeah? That was fast."

"I'm a P.I., I have resources."

He became so animated he almost straightened up. "No way! That's like really cool. Can you, like, shoot people and stuff?"

"No one can shoot people," I said, annoyed.

"Bummer."

He looked so disappointed I felt compelled to add: "I have pepper spray."

"Yeah? Do you have, like, any interesting cases?"

"Just cheating spouses and a stolen dog," I said with a shrug.

"Who's it stolen from?"

"That's the thing, we don't know."

"So how do you know it's stolen?"

"We have the dog. We have criminals coming after him. We just don't know who he belongs to or why he was stolen."

"I bet I could find out."

I gave him a dubious look. "How?"

"With a creative data search."

"Is it legal?"

He mulled the question. "Probably not." He glanced around. "Do you have a computer?"

I got up and fetched my battered laptop that was a hand-me-down from Jessica. Jarod gave it one look and huffed. "I'll have to set you up with proper equipment. I can't work like this."

"Don't you have a computer?"

He slumped, morose. "My girlfriend broke everything I had with a baseball bat. She said I paid more attention to computers than her." I could absolutely believe that, and kind of understood her too. He got up, full of purpose now. "Come on."

"Where are we going?"

"To get you a proper computer." He gave me a look that said I was really slow not to figure it out.

"I can't afford one."

"Don't worry, it won't cost you anything."

A statement guaranteed to make me worry. But I decided to protest later and just followed him out.

We took the subway to Dumbo, an area by the East River in north Brooklyn. It was a bit of a hassle with two line changes, because there was no direct line there from the station nearest to my home. Despite its name it was the hottest area in Kings County. It didn't used to be, but a developer had got his hands on the place and changed it into a hub of art and tech startups.

Lexton Security had its base of operations on Jay Street, near the Manhattan Bridge, only a short walk from the station past old warehouses and factories turned lofts and artists' studios. There were two bars on the street with music blaring from their open doors and customers milling in and out. Each place was trying to outdo the other with some sort of post-ironic industrial slash slum chic, and the customers were so hip it made my head hurt. I'd waited tables in a place like those, the only job I'd quit voluntarily, after two weeks.

Our destination was an erstwhile two story redbrick factory turned into open plan offices. Jarod had explained on our way here that the company had recently upgraded their office laptops—the ones the secretaries and accountants and such used—and he had salvaged a few of the old ones and they were waiting for him in his office. While most businesses on the street had closed for the night, the lights were still on in there.

"It's the nightshift," Jarod explained, as he swiped his identity card through the slot by the door and led us in.

"Cybercrime doesn't look at the time, especially the non-domestic cybercrime."

"So you're kind of a detective too?"

He looked delighted. "I guess I am. I just never come face to face with the people committing the crimes." He gave it a thought. "Which I think is good."

A security check later—people didn't just walk into a security firm—I followed Jarod through an industrial-strength steel door to bare concrete steps that led below ground. At their base was another steel door. A wave of heat and noise blasted at me when he opened it, staggering me. The sight that met my eyes was even more staggering.

The entire open basement was packed side to side with huge computer servers, miles and miles of cable running from them in thick clumps through the floor and ceiling. Air-conditioning and huge fans were blasting on full—hence the noise—but they couldn't quite counter the heat generated by the servers. And that on top of a cooling system of pipes that ran beneath the floor, into which cold water was fed straight from the East River, as Jarod explained to me once we could talk again.

We walked the entire length of the basement, me with hands on my ears, into a small, windowless room at the other end. The noise cut instantly when Jarod closed the door. It was considerably cooler too.

"That was unpleasant." I was sweaty after the relatively short walk and shivered in the cooler air of the small space.

"I've got used to it," Jarod answered distractedly, firing up a couple of computers and sitting down.

I watched him, baffled. "I thought we'd only fetch the computers."

"This is better. Unless you have a hundred gigabyte broadband connection?"

"I sometimes steal Wi-Fi from my neighbor."

Jarod rolled his eyes. "So, what are we looking for?"

I took a seat next to him and gave it a thought. "A criminal court judge or someone from the DA's office who owns a dog."

"Okay, so we need a list of their personnel first." It didn't take him long to get it. It was public data and his computers were incredibly fast. He was amazingly focused too, now that he had his computers. A different guy entirely.

"Now we go through their social media accounts. People with dogs are bound to post photos of them."

I wouldn't have come to think of that.

He worked on two displays at the same time, I on just one, and we had one more between us that showed the list of names we were searching. It was an education on what not to publish on social media, and that was just the public accounts. The stuff Jarod was able to find that was supposedly private was insane. Surely civil servants should know better.

"I could really use that skill," I told him, impressed. A P.I. could get a lot of useful information from people's private Facebook posts.

"The power can only be trusted to few."

Okay...

Maybe it was for the better. I'd only spy on Scott if I was given the chance, and that wasn't healthy.

A staggering number of the personnel owned pets, and since Jarod didn't know what Pippin looked like, I had to go through all the dog photos he found. Even with the special speed broadband at our disposal, it took almost an hour to hit the jackpot.

"Here he is!" The owner had Pippin's picture as his profile photo even. "No wonder Douglas's men were able to figure out where to hit hardest."

The owner was Daniel Thorne, Assistant DA for Kings County. I found it impressive, especially at only thirty-three—although Travis had managed the same in the defender services. But he kept his personal information private, so I learned nothing more of him, not even what he looked like. All his public photos were of Pippin.

"Do you want me to find his address?"

"Nah. It's late, so we can't go there tonight anyway. I'll e-mail the name to my boss and we'll contact him tomorrow." It would be best not to face the assistant DA with the knowledge that I'd hacked into his Facebook account. "Let's just go home now."

We couldn't leave before Jarod had gathered his computers. He stuffed three laptops into a sturdy canvas laundry bag that was lying in the corner. A useless item with him, but handy for carrying the laptops.

"I need your belt."

Baffled, I gave it to him, and he wrapped it around the bag, securing the laptops against each other so they wouldn't move inside and break. It was incredible how much attention he could pay to inanimate objects compared to how little attention he paid to his own wellbeing.

Cool air from the East River at the end of the street hit me when we got out, refreshing after the basement. We set a brisk pace—well, brisk-ish, as Jarod's only speed was ambling—past the revelers, ignoring drunken calls to join the party. Still a bit paranoid, I half expected someone to jump at us during the short walk. The wide, dark underpasses right before the subway station were especially unnerving. So when my phone rang just as we were about to go into the station, it startled me badly.

I paused to fumble out my phone—a complicated operation as I first had to put the pepper spray back into my pocket—and answer. "Why are you calling me at this hour?" I asked Jackson by way of greeting.

"Why are you sending me this kind of e-mail at this hour?" he countered. "Where the hell did you get the info?"

"His Facebook account. He has Pippin as his profile photo."

He was silent for a long heartbeat. "I wouldn't have come to think of that."

I wouldn't have either, but he sounded so admiring I wasn't about to confess it. "I had help."

"Jarod?"

"Not much of a guess, is it."

"Is he reliable?"

"Reliable enough for his bosses." Though I suspected they didn't really know what he used their ultrafast broadband for.

"Okay, then. Good job. I'll see you tomorrow." And he hung up.

A hand grabbed my shoulder.

Chapter Seventeen

I SWIVELED AROUND WITH A SHRIEK that echoed in the underpass, and shoved my phone forward as if it was the pepper spray. Good thing it wasn't, because Detective Lonny Peters, still dressed in his rumpled suit, would've got a face-full in that case. It would have served him right, though, for frightening me like that.

"You're out late," he said.

My mind blank, I struggled to come up with anything sensible. "Are you working? Nothing serious I hope?"

I eyed the entrance to the station with longing. Jarod was nowhere in sight. He must have gone down the steps while I was talking on the phone.

"No, just cruising. Do you need a lift home?" He indicated a large black SUV that was idling right next to us. Had it been there a moment earlier? Surely I would've noticed.

Then again, I had been talking on the phone.

"Thanks." I only barely managed to make it sound sincere. "But I've a friend waiting."

"He can come too."

Had he seen Jarod with me? The notion that he'd kept an eye on me made a shiver of fear run down my spine. Or maybe it was his tone. His words were so matter of fact—a good cop would offer a ride at this time of night, right?—yet I felt threatened by him. I don't know why, when I had found him so jovial earlier, but I wasn't willing to get into his car, with or without Jarod.

"Really, we're good."

"I'm afraid I have to insist."

"You do?" I asked baffled. "What for?"

"So we can go get the dog."

"What dog?" At that moment I honestly couldn't remember, even though I'd just spent an hour searching for him.

"The one you found," he said with a smile that seemed more sinister than amused.

"We placed him into foster care." I was proud I could remember that detail with how sluggish my brain was.

"I know. And you're going to show me where."

He pulled out a gun from his pocket and pointed it at me. I'd never been held at gunpoint and couldn't quite fathom the gravity of the situation. It was as if I were in a movie all of a sudden.

"I don't know their address." My eyes kept switching their focus between the weapon and Lonnie's face that was now devoid of all joviality.

"I find that hard to believe."

"Honestly. I only started at the agency yesterday and don't know where Jackson placed him." Not entirely a lie, since I didn't know where Cheryl lived. "You'll have to ask him."

He stared at me for a pregnant moment. "Then we'll do that. Together." He opened the back door of the car and pointed with the gun for me to get in. Out of options, that's what I did, stumbling a little as I climbed to the high backseat. Lonnie gave me a boost from my bottom, making my skin crawl.

We weren't alone in the car. Lonnie took the backseat with me, and in the driver's seat was Jonny Moreira. Seeing the big guy drove in the seriousness of the situation much better than Lonnie's gun had.

"You're working for Craig Douglas?" I asked Lonnie, barely believing it. It hadn't even occurred to me. Though, in hindsight, why else would he have been interested in the dog?

"It's the only sensible option. He's going to rule the place, and anyone getting in his way is utterly foolish."

"And you're trying to get to his good graces by finding the dog?" It came out more mocking than I intended, but really it was absurd. The gun turned back to point at me.

"Just tell us where to find your boss."

A moment of panic seized my innards because I didn't know Jackson's address either, but then I remembered: "He's staying at the office because the door is broken."

Moreira's hands tightened on the steering wheel, as if he was trying to curb his anger. Lonnie was openly furious. "We have to get that fucking retard Costa for it."

"For breaking in and revealing Moreira had been there?"

"Yes. What's the point in sending in a pro if amateurs then wreck everything," Lonnie spat. Moreira's anger seemed to intensify too, but I got a curious notion it was for Lonnie's words. I guess he didn't want to be publicly identified as a professional B&E guy.

"Not if we get him first," I said, not even knowing where I got the courage to taunt Lonnie. I should be terrified. His lifted the gun to point at my face and I raised my hands, calming. "Hey, I need the money."

The fairly short drive passed in silence after that. I had tons of questions I wanted to know, like had Lonnie worked for MacRath too? Was the whole precinct rotten or just him? And what had they thought to accomplish by stealing an assistant DA's dog. But it was finally starting to sink in that I was in mortal danger, and so I kept my mouth shut.

I briefly entertained the idea of escaping at a stoplight, but with my luck the two men would be in better shape than me and would easily catch me. Well, Moreira would be anyway. He was big but it was all muscle. I didn't cherish the idea of being chased by him in the dark. Or maybe he wouldn't chase me, he would just shoot me.

I pretty much stopped breathing altogether after that thought hit me.

When Moreira pulled over outside the agency, I exited the car without a word, and though my legs twitched when I passed the steps to the subway, as if I contemplated diving down, I just walked to the entrance door. There a new problem halted us. The door was locked.

"I don't have the key."

"What sort of boss doesn't give his underlings a key?" Lonnie asked, incredulous.

"I told you, I only started yesterday."

Moreira didn't say a word. If I hadn't talked to him the other day, I would've thought he couldn't speak. He just pulled out a small square metal case, thin like a cigar box, from the inner pocket of his jacket, and opened it to reveal a selection of lockpicks. Despite the seriousness of the situation, I watched with fascinated interest how he opened the lock with only a few moves, almost as fast as if he'd used a key.

"That's a handy skill," I said, admiring, when he pushed the door open. His mouth quirked in answer. "Really. I could use it myself." Maybe Jackson could teach me.

"You're not allowed to break into peoples' homes," he said, sounding oddly like Jackson when he tried to teach me the trade.

"That's a funny thing for a professional breaking and entering guy to say."

But Moreira just pointed at me to get in and then turned to head to his car. I panicked.

"You're not leaving me alone with him, are you?" Of the two men, Moreira seemed more levelheaded. Weird I know, but he wasn't here to impress a new boss. There was something desperate about Lonnie, which might lead to rash action. With a gun.

With me at the wrong end of the barrel.

"He's not going to harm you," he said, but didn't seem to believe his words, because he gave Lonnie a glare that didn't promise him anything good if he did harm me.

Lonnie didn't say anything, but just pushed me in. I walked ahead of him to the elevator, conscious of his gun directed at my back. It made my spine tighten in fear and I had trouble breathing, my heart hammering in my chest. The ride to the second floor was mercifully brief, as I feared I would faint for lack of oxygen. I didn't even have enough breath to shout to give Jackson a warning when we exited the elevator. It was close to hyper-ventilating.

Outside the agency door, Lonnie grabbed a hold of me and thrust the gun painfully against my side. "Just in case Jackson isn't willing to see reason," he said. Then he kicked the already broken door open and pushed me in before him.

Things happened so fast I had trouble comprehending what went down. Lonnie was yanked to the side from behind me with such force that he didn't even have time to fire his gun. A moment later he was lying face first on the floor, disarmed and with his hands cuffed behind his back.

"Don't move," Jackson ordered Lonnie with a hard voice. He went to the door, a gun trained at Lonnie the whole time.

"Moreira's downstairs," I managed to say, and he disappeared.

I sat on the floor.

Okay, I slumped to the floor, my knees giving up on me. It brought me annoyingly close to Lonnie's face, but I couldn't muster enough energy to care.

"He's gone," Jackson said when he returned a few minutes later.

"Why? How? I mean, how would he know you'd catch Lonnie?"

He glanced at the detective. "I think this was a setup. For him."

"What?" Lonnie and I exclaimed simultaneously.

"I received an anonymous call only moments before you came in. Very likely from Moreira."

"Why?"

"Cleanup of the old regime I'd say."

Lonnie was so livid he looked like he was having a stroke. "That's not true," he spat, trying to turn on his back, but he was a bit too portly to manage the maneuver with his hands tied to his back. "They need me."

"You won't be any use for them once you've lost your job."

"My guys will free me the moment you call them to fetch me."

"I guess we won't call your boys, then," Jackson said calmly. "Perhaps someone from my old precinct still owes me a favor." He took out a phone.

"This is your fault," Lonnie said to me.

I stared at him, too tired to do anything else. "This has nothing to do with me. I bet Douglas feared MacRath would rat out his contacts during the trial, if he hasn't already. He couldn't trust you."

That still didn't quite explain why Moreira would've called Jackson, but I was too tired to care or wonder about the workings of the criminal mind.

Chapter Eighteen

JACKSON ENDED HIS PHONE CALL and came to me. "Come, let's get you on the sofa." He helped me up and to his office. I wasn't even embarrassed that my feet wouldn't carry me properly and he had to support me. I'd been held at gunpoint. It was a wonder I hadn't wet myself.

"Do you need a nip of whiskey?"

"Yes, please." I dropped onto the couch, the lovely, safe couch. There was a pillow and a blanket on it—I guess this wasn't the first time Jackson had slept here—and I took the blanket and wrapped it around me. I would never get up. Jackson could sleep on the floor for all I cared, without the blanket, because I was keeping it.

Jackson went to a cupboard at the side of the room and pulled out a bottle and a glass. He poured me a hefty dose that would put me under if I drank it all.

My hands were shaking and I had to concentrate on not spilling the contents when he handed me the glass. The first sip burned my throat, making me cough. Second sip went down slightly better, and by the third it was like drinking water. The whiskey made my blood course faster and warmed me all over. It was tempting to drink it all and welcome the oblivion it offered, but I wanted to be sober when the police arrived.

I don't know how long I'd sat there in silence when Jackson spoke at the door, cutting into my contemplation of the floor pattern. "Can you keep an eye on this piece of shit while I go let the cops in?" He was assessing me, and I tried to look sharp and capable.

"Absolutely." My voice slurred a little. "What should I do if he tries to escape?"

"You have the pepper spray, don't you?"

I dug into the pocket of my sweater jacket and pulled it out. "Yep."

My feet were only slightly tottering as I walked to the reception room. Lonnie was still on the floor, but Jackson had helped him upright and he was leaning against the wall, sulking. I kind of wished he would give me trouble; my finger was practically itching to release the pepper spray. But he wouldn't even look at me.

Jackson returned with two uniformed officers, both sturdy, hard-looking men who gave Lonnie such an ugly glare that I had no doubt he would end up behind bars. But they weren't the only ones arriving. Following at their heels was my brother.

Trevor didn't even glance at Lonnie. He came straight to me, full of concern, and pulled me into a hug. All the tension I'd bottled was released and I started crying.

"Are you hurt?" he asked, worried, holding me tighter.

"No, just relieved," I said past my sobs.

"What the hell happened?"

I pulled myself together and wiped my eyes on the sleeve of my sweater. I watched Lonnie being escorted out by the officers—not very gently—and I waved my hand towards him. "I think he followed me tonight. He attacked me outside York Street station and forced me into his car at gunpoint."

"What the fuck for?" Trevor's hand twitched, as if he were reaching for his sidearm to shoot Lonnie. Luckily the asshole was out of sight already or he might've actually done it.

"He wanted Pippin."

He stared at me amazed. "I think you'd better tell me everything."

So I did. I hadn't even told Jackson the whole story yet, so both men listened, interested.

"Why were you in Dumbo in the first place?"

Since Trevor didn't know about Jarod, I had to tell that story too, which took considerably longer, as—predictably—he wasn't too happy about my decision to take a housemate without consulting him.

"Jackson ran a background check for me," I said defensively, but that only made Trevor direct his ire at him.

"And you! You were supposed to keep my sister safe. And here she is, on her second day, being held at gunpoint."

"What do you mean, he was supposed to keep me safe?" I asked, annoyed. "You didn't issue him ultimatums, did you?"

"Of course I did. And he promised to give you only easy cases."

It was my turn to glare at Jackson. He didn't even have the sense to look sheepish. "It was an easy case. A lost dog, for Christ's sake. We couldn't possibly know criminals would be interested in Pippin."

"I don't need babysitting," I huffed, but to my aggravation it only made Jackson smile.

"Of course you do. You've only just started. You know nothing about this job."

"And now she won't, because she'll quit," Trevor announced, as if he had the right to dictate what I do.

"I will do no such thing!"

My brother gave me his best hard stare. He was getting better at it, but his high-handed declaration had miffed me, so I was immune to it.

"Yes you will. It's not safe for you here."

"You can't tell me what to do."

"I'm your brother and I know what's best for you."

"Like you decided it was best for me not to know Scott is back in town?"

"It would've only hurt you."

"And having my brother keep things from me wouldn't?"

He had the good sense to blush at least. "I made a decision not to let him back into your life."

"I'm a grown woman and I make my own decisions," I said, raising my voice considerably.

Trevor huffed. "You haven't made a grownup decision in your life."

That stung. Big time.

"Well, then, keeping this job will be the first one, and you'll stay out of it!"

"If I may intervene," Jackson said, and we both swiveled on him so fast he lifted his hands in placating manner. "Admittedly, this has been quite a day for Tracy, but it isn't normally this exciting in this job. We'll get Pippin back to his owner tomorrow, and then we'll return to trailing unfaithful spouses."

Trevor glowered, not willing to change his mind, so I linked my arm around his, placating. "I really want to keep this job. I haven't felt this alive in years. I can't go back to waitressing. I'd die there."

He didn't look convinced, but he nodded, reluctantly. "Fine. But the moment people start shooting at you, you're out."

"If that ever happens, I'll probably want to quit myself."

He put an arm around me and gave me a brief hug. "Let's get you home, then. It's getting really late."

Jackson patted me on the shoulder. "Good job today. I'll see you in the morning and we'll take Pippin to his owner together."

I smiled. "Thanks. And thank you for saving my life." I pushed Trevor out the door before he would take another exception with my words.

The drive home was quiet. Trevor didn't try to talk me into changing my mind, but I could see he was still troubled by my decision. I could live with that, as long as he didn't try to control my life. I didn't want to think of what he'd said about me. My family had been saying the same thing for years, ever since I quit college to marry Scott, only to divorce a year later. But now that I'd finally taken a step toward changing my life, I wanted them to support me.

"There's no need to tell Dad about this, is there?" I asked when he pulled over outside my building. "He'd only worry."

Trevor nodded, looking grim. "I won't talk. But you've got to stay safe, you hear me."

I leaned over to hug him. "I promise." He waited until I'd got into the building before driving away.

Jarod was sitting on the hallway floor, leaning against the wall, fast asleep. I felt embarrassed for having completely forgotten about him, but at least he had made it home safely. I shook him lightly by the shoulder and he woke up.

"Hey! You made it," he said, delighted, looking bleary. "I was, like, afraid when that guy pulled out a gun."

I led us in. "Sorry about that. This job turned out to be more exciting than I thought." Utterly beat, I went to my room and fell face-first on the bed. I was instantly asleep.

I woke up when the phone started buzzing in my pocket. It was a wonder I hadn't crushed it, but as I pushed myself to a more upright position I realized I hadn't moved the whole night. The display told me it was Tessa calling and the alarm clock on the nightstand that it was seven in the morning. I was instantly worried.

"Hey, has something happened?"

"No," she answered calmly, if slightly puzzled. "Why would you ask that?"

"Why are you calling me this early, then?"

"Aren't you usually up and at work at this hour?"

"I'm not a waitress anymore, so no. What's up?" I could barely keep the annoyance from my voice.

"Have you showed Richard the photos yet?"

It took me a moment to remember who he was and what photos she was talking about. The events of the previous night had completely wiped the amazing revelation of her affair from my mind.

"No."

"Good, because Angela's changed her mind. She wants to talk to him herself." She sounded miffed, clearly not understanding such sentimentalism.

"Okay, I'll see what I can do."

"You mean you won't do it?"

"I didn't say that. But we work for Richard, not you."

"Well, do your best. This needs to be handled delicately."

"I'm surprised you know the concept."

"Angela made me understand that Mom and Dad won't necessarily take it lightly that I'm dating a woman."

Weren't we a pair, trying to keep things from our parents.

"If Trevor's reaction is anything to go by, then no."

"You told him?"

Her piqued tone made me realize she hadn't necessarily wanted him to know about her relationship either. "Yes," I confessed, apologetic. "I'm sorry."

She was quiet for a heartbeat. "Well, that's one thing less to worry about." And she hung up.

Chapter Nineteen

MY SECOND EARLY MORNING phone call came when I was having breakfast. "I ran into Suzy Carter's mother on my morning jog," Trevor said. I suppressed a shudder thinking of the words "morning" and "jog" in connection—or separate for that matter.

"She said Suzy and Moreira have been going out for only a couple of weeks, and that he's such a nice young man."

"Nice?" I was intimidated by him before he even spoke. Last night's events hadn't exactly changed my opinion of him.

"Her words. Helps around the house and drives them to church."

I failed to wrap my mind around that image.

"Did she tell you how they met?"

"No, but knowing Moreira's connection to MacRath, it's not hard to guess."

"At least my ex isn't a drug dealer," I said, with feeling. Scott had had his failings, but he wasn't a criminal. Although, being a scumbag should be made a criminal offence in my opinion.

"Or your current boyfriend."

"I don't have a current boyfriend," I reminded him.

"Shouldn't you try to get over Scott by now?"

"I'm over him." But it didn't come out as resolute as I intended.

He sighed. "Right... Well, I'll keep an eye on Suzy's house. We'll get Moreira."

His words didn't make me feel as good as they should have. "He was just the driver. And he warned Jackson about Lonnie." In my mind, Lonnie was the real criminal here.

"He hurt you. He'll pay."

"That's just it. I don't feel hurt by him. But I wouldn't leave me alone with Lonnie." My hands itched to strangle him.

That made Trevor laugh. "I'm not making any promises about Moreira."

"Just as long as you're not going after him to get even with Suzy."

"Not hardly," he huffed. "I was over her before school was out."

"You're stronger than me, then."

"I wasn't in love with her."

As I'd been with Scott. But that went unsaid.

Jarod ambled into the kitchen wearing only boxer briefs, a sight that I could do without, especially on a beanpole like him. "I have to, like, go to work," he said, going to the fridge, when I wondered why he was awake so early.

I opened a kitchen drawer and pulled out a key. I might as well give it to him. It wasn't like I'd throw him out.

"Here. Use it responsibly. Meaning, no filling the house with unsavory friends."

He took the key, but gave it an apprehensive look. "I'm not sure I have friends."

I stared at him stunned. "What? Everyone has friends, from work or from college."

Though come to think of it, I hadn't formed close friendships during my one year at college, and every time I'd switched jobs I'd lost the friends I'd made in the previous job, though new ones had always filled their place. Then I'd had Jessica, but I hadn't heard from her since she moved out.

Some friend she turned out to be.

"I'm, like, younger than those who are intelligent enough to hang out with and we have nothing in common, or find those my age too stupid to bother with."

I could actually see that.

"Well, we can be each other's home friends."

He smiled and it transformed his face. "That would be cool."

Before I managed to leave for work, I got my third call of the morning, this one from Jackson. “I’ll come pick you up. We’ll meet Cheryl at the DA’s office. She’ll bring Pippin. No need to give anyone a chance to intercept us this close to the goal.”

I was waiting for him outside my building when Moreira’s huge car pulled over by the curb. I looked around for the fastest safe place to run to, but he was out of his car before I could make my legs move. Just the same, I couldn’t have outrun him anyway. I dug out my pepper spray instead and pointed it at him when he approached me.

He lifted his hands. “I’m not here to cause trouble.”

“Yeah, right. I don’t have the dog and I wouldn’t give him to you even if I had.”

“I don’t care about the dog. It’s Douglas’s private matter.”

“Then why did you abduct me last night?”

He shrugged his muscled shoulders. “Lonnie was so eager to get to you, that I thought it best to tag along so he wouldn’t get carried away.”

“And then you left me alone with him.” I was truly incensed.

“I did call Dean and warn him. Don’t I get points for that?” His smile was disarming, but I hardened myself.

“You did it just so you could get rid of Lonnie. You’ll get a face full of pepper spray, that’s what you get for scaring the shit out of me.”

"Sorry about that."

He sounded so sincere my anger deflated. "Yeah, well, just don't let it happen again. And stay away from my brother. He'll shoot you on sight."

"As will Dean, I'd wager." He nodded towards my boss's car, which was approaching pretty fast. "I'll see you around." And he got into his car and drove away just as Jackson surged out of his car, a gun in his hand. I half expected him to fire after Moreira's car, but he curbed his anger, put the weapon away and rounded the car to me instead.

"Did he hurt you?"

"No. And I had my pepper spray ready." Which I still hadn't had a chance to use. We got in the car and were on the move.

"What did he want?"

"If I didn't know better, I'd say to apologize."

"Good thing you know better, then."

"Yeah. He told me that Pippin is Douglas's private project."

"Makes sense, if he wants to free his brother-in-law."

"That's just it. Why would he want to do that?"

He gave me a sharp glance. "You mean because he's taking over MacRath's territory."

"Yes. It would be in his best interest to make sure MacRath stays behind bars."

"Perhaps blood is more important than business."

I had to concede that. Then I took a closer look at him. "You've changed clothes." With his black on black ensemble it wasn't easy to tell, but he had clearly showered and shaved. His hair was damp and he smelled nice. Pine and leather.

"Yeah, I popped home in the early hours of the morning."

"Is it far?"

"Marine Park." It was southeast from Midwood, right by Jamaica Bay. "I own a small semi there, not far from the park. Good place for running." He gave me a meaningful glance, which I took to indicate he intended me to take up running too.

Maybe tomorrow. Or next week.

"What else do we have scheduled for today besides this delivery?" I asked, ignoring his hint.

"Mr. Jenkins is coming over this morning."

I remembered Tessa's call. "My sister asked that we don't show the photos to Mr. Jenkins after all."

"Oh?"

"Apparently Angela, Mrs. Jenkins, wants to deal with the matter herself."

"What does she suggest we tell our client? We have to eat too, you know."

I gave it a thought. "The truth. That we kept an eye on the house and didn't see any man go there while he was gone."

Jackson blinked. Then he started laughing. "That might actually work. I'll think about it."

After about a week in traffic, we reached the huge modern skyscraper in Downtown, Brooklyn, that housed the DA's office—and a Marriot hotel too, of all things odd. Jackson drove us into the parking garage underneath the building. It was pretty full already, even that early in the morning, so it took us a while to find a free spot. Then it was a matter of locating Cheryl and Pippin, which Jackson handled by calling her.

"Tracy, you take Pippin, and Cheryl, you go back to the office," Jackson instructed us when we reached her car. "Someone needs to keep an eye on it until the door repairmen come."

I rounded Cheryl's car to the front passenger seat, where Pippin was sitting, wearing some sort of neoprene harness—pink, naturally—that secured him to the seatbelt. He looked satisfied with himself. Maybe his owner wouldn't let him sit in the front seat.

He was delighted to see me and expressed himself with jumping and barking, which echoed loudly in the garage. I feared that the bad guys would hear us, so I tried to quiet him. Moreira hadn't followed us—that I'd noticed—but you never knew with these things. Fortunately Pippin calmed down quickly.

"It's so sad to see him go," Cheryl sighed, tears in her eyes. "We had such wonderful times together, didn't we." She leaned over to pet and kiss Pippin one more time.

"I'm sad too, but we can't let the bad guys win."

I extracted Pippin from the seatbelt and lifted him in my arms. He wasn't happy about being carried, but I wasn't going to take any risks. Glancing left and right, certain that we'd be ambushed, I hurried side by side with Jackson to the elevator. I would see Pippin to his owner even if was the last thing I did.

Chapter Twenty

THE ELEVATOR FILLED ALREADY on the next floor, pushing us to the back of the car. I held Pippin tighter, but these people were only interested in their phones and morning papers, not in him. No one even noted how cute he looked.

Pippin, for his part, was infinitely curious about everyone and everything. Especially interesting was the long, flowing hair of the woman standing right in front of us, which he kept nibbling the whole ride. I didn't have enough room to pull him away, so perhaps it was for the best that the people ignored him.

We reached the correct floor and were spewed out at the bland government-style lobby of the district attorney's offices. People were still arriving to their stations and we slipped in among them, skipping the reception desk, and headed down a long hallway pretty much unnoticed. I would've expected slightly tighter security.

There were offices on both sides of the hallway and we read the nametags to locate the correct one. But before we'd found it, Pippin became really animated and managed to free himself from my arms. He jumped down and in through the door of the nearest office. Trying to catch him before he did any damage, I dove after him.

Only to bang my head against the stomach of the person about to exit the office.

"What the hell?" a man exclaimed, not even slightly winded for the contact.

I rubbed my forehead as I took a look at who I'd smashed into. A furious man, for one; fit, for another. Those abs hadn't given an inch. Tall. Even after I straightened I had to keep looking up. Incredibly handsome. Pretty almost. There was a slight curl to his short, light brown hair and his bright blue eyes were framed by lashes so long I'd need falsies to achieve the same.

"Sorry." I had to blink. "I tried to catch the dog."

Pippin was ecstatic, running a tight circle around the man's legs and yapping. He gave the dog a baffled look and frowned.

"Is this my dog?" He realized that underneath all the pink was his pet and a smile lit his face, melting what few brain cells I had left after the impact he'd made, both physical and mental.

"There you are." He leaned down and lifted Pippin into his arms, allowing the dog to lick his face. Yuck. "Where have you been all this time, you naughty boy? I've been so worried."

The man and the dog spent a few moments happily reuniting. Then he shot a piercing glance at me that wasn't dampened by the pretty lashes.

"What are you doing with my dog? And what the hell is he wearing?"

I wanted to answer him. I really did. But for the life of me I couldn't make my scrambled brain restart. Jackson cleared his throat.

"This is your show, Tracy."

"Huh? Right... " But all I saw were the pretty eyes of Daniel Thorne, Assistant DA. Because that's who he had to be.

"I found your dog a couple of days ago," I managed to say.

"Couple of days? Where?"

"He showed up at the Café Marina in Prospect Heights."

"Prospect Heights? I don't live anywhere near there. And why did you wait this long to bring him back?"

"He wasn't wearing a collar so we didn't know who he belonged to."

He gave me a slow look. "He has a microchip."

"A what?"

"An identification chip planted under his skin. Any vet could've checked him for you."

I looked at Jackson again, who shrugged. "He looked like a mongrel so I thought he wouldn't have one."

"You're Jackson Dean, aren't you?" Mr. Thorne asked.

"What do you have to do with this?"

Jackson wasn't as taken with Thorne's pretty face—go figure—so he just nodded. "It's a bit of a story, and it has to do with the MacRath case."

"MacRath case? I'm not on it."

We were both stunned by his statement, but it was Jackson who spoke. I still hadn't found my tongue. "You're not? Then why the hell was your dog stolen by his brother-in-law?"

Thorne was utterly bewildered. "What? I thought my ex had taken him to put pressure on the settlement negotiations we're starting today." He blushed lightly, which I found adorable. "I guess I owe her an apology."

"May I ask who your ex is?" I was proud it came out clear and without sighs.

He frowned at me. "Why?"

I fought the brain-melting effects of his face to gather my thoughts. "It makes absolutely no sense for anyone to steal an assistant DA's dog to put pressure on him in a high-profile case, especially if he's even not on it. Even less so if that someone is about to take over the drug business left vacant by said case. But it does make sense for your ex to steal him." I'd have done the same if Scott had had anything worth fighting over.

"So is she by any chance from New Jersey?"

"Are you saying Patricia would've hired someone to steal Mac?" he asked incredulous.

"Is that his name? I call him Pippin," I said, delighted, and felt a poke in my side. Jackson.

"Concentrate."

"Right. Yes, that's what I'm saying. Craig Douglas, or someone working for him stole him for her."

"Allegedly stole."

That's lawyers for you.

Daniel—I'd definitely call him by his first name, or Danny—blinked his beautiful lashes at me. "Yes. She's from New Jersey. But it's really farfetched."

I shrugged. "Worth checking out, I'd say."

He got a gleam in his eyes that didn't promise anything good for his ex-wife. "I believe I shall."

"We'd be happy to offer our services," Jackson said and I nodded eagerly. Daniel ran his fingers through his hair, and I'm not entirely sure what was said after that.

Jackson snapped his fingers in front of my eyes. "Earth to Tracy." I blinked. Daniel and Pippin—Mac—had disappeared without me noticing. They'd even managed to strip the dog and Jackson was holding the pink accessories. He snorted a laugh. "Man, the pretty boy really got to you."

"Sooo pretty." I followed him down the hallway and back to the elevator. "Where are we going?" It made him laugh harder.

"You didn't hear a word, did you?"

"Nope." And I wasn't even embarrassed.

"First we'll go to the office to meet with Richard Jenkins." The reminder was like a cold shower and brought me back to reality. "Then we'll have a chat with Daniel Thorne's soon to be ex mother-in-law."

"In New Jersey?"

"No, luckily she's staying with her daughter during this 'trying time.'" He made air quotes with his fingers. "Her words, not Thorne's."

"But won't the daughter be there?"

"She's at work."

The drive to the agency was short. Cheryl got tears in her eyes when I gave Pippin's leash and collar back to her. "He looked so pretty in them."

"I know. But he was very happy to stay with his owner. His name was Mac."

"I'll always think of him as Pippin."

"Me too." I told her what we had learned and she immediately began searching for everything she could find on the soon to be former Mrs. Thorne's mother.

I left her to it when my phone rang. It was Tessa again.

"Angela changed her mind. You can show Richard the photos."

"Are you sure? He'll be here any minute now and then it'll be too late."

I heard her relay my words to Angela, and her answer too, but it was Tessa who spoke.

"Yes."

"Okay. He's here now," I said, spying him entering reception. "I got to go."

Jackson gave me a questioning look. "We'll use the photos?"

"Yes. Angela changed her mind."

"Very good."

I studied Richard Jenkins as he entered the office, feeling curious and apprehensive. He was the key to my sister's happiness. He was in his mid-thirties and wore an expensive business suit. He looked uptight, but so would I if I were about to hear whether or not my husband was cheating on me. Or wife, in his case. It didn't help my mood that she was, and that I'd provided the evidence myself.

This would surely be the first of many similar meetings to come, so I settled in to watch how Jackson handled it. He greeted the man as he did everyone, with a firm handshake and a direct look in the eyes, not indicating in any way what was to come.

"Well?" Mr. Jenkins asked the moment he had sat down—on the edge of his seat. This mattered to him, and I felt for him. I glanced at Jackson, hoping he had noticed the same, and he nodded calmly at me.

"My apprentice and I spent three evenings outside your house while you were gone. Your wife was home every evening, and there were no men visiting her."

Mr. Jenkins relaxed visibly and I wasn't sure if it was good after all. It would make the truth feel that much worse. Jackson seemed to agree, because he continued:

"However, she wasn't alone." Mr. Jenkins stiffened again. "Each night a woman came to visit, and she stayed the whole night."

"How would you know?"

"I returned every morning to wait for her to leave."

I hadn't known that.

"A friend of hers?" Mr. Jenkins asked hopefully. He glanced at me, as if seeking for confirmation.

"I think you need to prepare yourself for the idea that your wife is having an affair with another woman," I said as kindly as I could. He pulled back, stunned.

"How dare you say that?"

"Would it be any different if it were a man?"

"Yes, of course it would be. I'm sure the woman is just a friend and you're trying to slander my wife. I will not have that."

He was furious now, a disproportional reaction to our news, as if it mattered more to her reputation that she was gay than whether or not she was having an affair. Or maybe he feared that it would reflect more badly on him that she was having an affair with a woman and he wasn't strong enough to handle it. There was barely contained violence in him even, and I debated the wisdom of showing him the photos after all. What if he attacked us? But it would be better if he did it here, than with Angela later. Jackson could defend us.

Besides, I still hadn't had a chance to use my pepper spray, which I'd itched to do these past two days.

Jackson turned his computer screen around so that Mr. Jenkins could see. "I have photos that will shock you, so, please, prepare yourself." But he didn't give Mr. Jenkins a chance before opening the first photo.

"What ... no, that's not my wife." But he took a closer look. After seeing all of them, he had to admit defeat. He looked deflated and a bit gray. "Who is she?"

"Her colleague from the hospital." I didn't want to admit the family connection.

"I see..." He seemed lost for a moment, but pulled himself together. His anger had returned, evident in how his fists kept opening and closing. "Thank you. Send me your invoice. And destroy those photos." He headed out of the door without a glance back.

I slumped in relief. "That went well enough."

"Yes."

I took out my phone and texted Tessa to tell the outcome. Then I called Trevor. "Can you do your sister a favor?"

"Which one?" he asked, teasing.

"Tessa. Her girlfriend's husband just learned about the affair and it might be good if Angela wasn't alone when he comes home."

"Is he violent?" he asked in a very different tone. It didn't promise anything good for Mr. Jenkins should he take his anger out on his wife.

"On the edge of it. Call Tessa."

I was exhausted, as if I'd been put through a wringer and stretched thin. "Any chance we can call it a day early?"

Jackson smiled. "No, but we'll have an early lunch. And then we'll go to meet Mrs. Allen."

Chapter Twenty-one

PATRICIA THORNE—AND HER mother, Mrs. Allen—lived in the couple's apartment in Brooklyn Heights, in a Victorian townhouse with an unobstructed view over the East River to the skyline of southern Manhattan. It was as prime a spot as you could get in Brooklyn, and I didn't wonder that the divorcing couple was fighting over the apartment.

Cheryl had dug up some details and we'd learned that the apartment had belonged to Mr. Thorne's family for ages—he came from old money—but since he'd cheated on his wife—which immediately doused my undying love for him—she had a good basis for claiming the place.

Though not good enough if she'd had to steal the dog.

The quiet street outside the building was empty, but Jackson chose a spot a little away from the house for the car. "We'll observe for a moment."

I sighed internally and settled to observe.

We observed a nanny leave the building with a toddler in a stroller—with great difficulty, as the granite steps up to the front door were steep and there was no ramp—and head toward the end of the building and the playground with the best view in all Brooklyn there. We observed a bus pull over and spew a horde of Japanese tourists with cameras from its guts to go take a few photos of Manhattan from the Brooklyn Heights Promenade. We observed a delivery van for an Italian restaurant pull over, the driver take a large box of food from the back and head with it to the house we were keeping an eye on.

"Is it just me, or does the delivery guy look a bit old?" I asked Jackson, having observed the curious detail.

"And is it just me, or is he trying really hard not to be recognized?" Jackson asked in return.

"I'd go even so far as to say he's embarrassed to be a delivery guy, or maybe it's just me again."

"It could be you, yes," Jackson said nodding, his sharp eyes trained on the man as he disappeared into the building. "But I'd say the guy looked a lot like Craig Douglas underneath that ball cap and fake mustache."

My heart skipped a beat. "What do you think this is about?"

"I have no idea, but it's not a coincidence he's here. He knows Mrs. Allen."

"But why the disguise?"

Jackson shrugged. "Maybe he's trying his best not to be connected with Mrs. Allen. He must suspect we've taken Mac to his owner, which means their game is up."

"Wouldn't it be easier to stay away then?"

"Yes it would. So the question becomes, what was in that container."

"Awful lot of food for just two people, that's what."

He grinned. "Let's go find out."

"How do you want to play this?"

"All we need is a proof that Douglas knows Thorne's mother-in-law."

"Meaning?"

"Meaning we'll take a photo of the two together."

Jackson took out a compact but effective-looking camera from the glove compartment. Then we got out of the car and crossed the street to the house. The front door was locked, to the surprise of no one. I sort of expected him to pull out lockpicks like Moreira had the previous night, but instead he turned to the buzzers by the door.

However, before he could select one, the nanny returned with the toddler, who was in the throes of an epic tantrum. Jackson hurried down the steps to carry the stroller up to the door and the grateful nanny opened the door without asking why we were there. Not that she would've heard the answer over the child's screaming.

She thanked us profusely as she crammed the stroller into the tiny, retrofitted elevator. "I'm sorry, but we can't all fit in."

I shuddered at the idea of sharing a ride with the loud

toddler, but Jackson just smiled. "That's okay. We can walk." The smile he got in return was openly inviting.

"You should've asked for her number," I said as we headed up the stairs. He gave me a funny look, so I hastened to add: "You're not married, are you?" Weird, how I hadn't thought to ask that before.

"No."

"So what was wrong with her? I thought she was pretty."

"She was twenty!"

"She was willing is all I'm saying."

We reached the correct floor. "You go first and try to look innocent," Jackson said with a low voice. Since I was wearing my fancy new butterfly clips again, I had the innocent part covered. "I'll stand out of sight."

I assumed my most guileless face, the one I used with extremely annoying customers to keep my cool, the face that said 'I'm too stupid to understand your demands': big eyes, and mouth slightly open as if in perpetual surprise. You'd be amazed how well it usually worked. I could keep it up much longer than annoying customers could pester me. Then I knocked on the door.

A dog began barking inside the apartment and I heard a woman order it sharply to shut up. High heels clicked against a hardwood floor and the door was opened by a woman in her early sixties—or well-preserved late sixties; she was so nipped and tucked it was hard to tell. Her dark brown hair was in a bouffant do and she had squeezed her voluptuous body into leopard print spandex.

I blinked, baffled, and opened my mouth to greet her when a man shouted from somewhere inside the apartment. "Don't let the dog run out!"

I looked down and saw a little dog much like Pippin—Mac—about to make a mad dash to freedom. Instinctively, I dropped on my knees and managed to capture the dog just as the man ran to the door too. Above me, a camera shutter closed with a click.

"Thank you," Jackson said, taking a few more photos. "I think this will be all."

Craig Douglas lunged towards Jackson and I scrambled up hastily, the dog tightly in my arms. The woman shrieked and flailed, trying to get out of his way, but she only managed to trip him and lose his balance. Jackson grabbed a hold of him and a moment later he was on his knees, handcuffed.

"You can't arrest me. I've done nothing wrong."

"You've stolen a dog, for starters," Jackson said calmly. "That's a plausible cause to hold you until the police arrive."

"That's my daughter's dog," Mrs. Allen said indignantly.

"She has two?" I asked, baffled, baffling the woman in return.

"Of course not. One of those horrible things is enough. Mac is his name. My cousin delivered him just now." She nodded towards Douglas, who was shooting daggers at her.

"Are you willing to go on record with it?" Jackson asked.

And when the woman said "Absolutely," he pulled out his phone and fired up the video, even though Douglas told her to shut up. Jackson nodded at me to ask my questions.

"So you're saying that Mr. Craig Douglas here is your cousin?"

"Yes."

"And he stole your daughter's dog?"

She frowned—or tried to anyway. Her brows weren't exactly mobile anymore. "He didn't steal anything, that's what I'm trying to tell you. He's my daughter's dog as much as it's her ex-husband's."

"So your daughter gave Mac to Douglas?"

"Yes."

"To be kept away from Mr. Thorne?"

"Yes."

"Shut the fuck up, Loreen," Douglas growled, startling the woman, but she wasn't done yet.

"And now he's brought the dog back, so you see, there's been no crime. You can't arrest him."

I fought valiantly not to grin. "I'm afraid Mr. Douglas hasn't been honest with you."

"What?"

"This isn't Mac."

"Of course he is."

I shook my head. "For one, we delivered Mac to Mr. Thorne this morning. For another..." I lifted the dog for her to take a closer look, "this one's a girl."

"What?" The woman pulled back, appalled.

"Your cousin probably failed to tell you that he let Mac run away and we found him. He tried to get Mac back, which helped us figure out who he belongs to. Having failed to fetch the real dog, he then delivered you this one." Probably in that food container he had carried in earlier.

Jackson barked a laugh. "What did you think to do? Take photos of the dog on today's paper to show Thorne that you have Mac so he would be more willing to negotiate? Don't you think he would've spotted the difference?"

"He's not getting this apartment," Mrs. Allen declared, getting angry again. "It belongs to my daughter."

"I think you just made the settlement negotiations that much more difficult for her."

I watched the woman realize she probably should have listened to Douglas after all. Her face distorted with fury. "Not if I get that phone," she hissed and made to grab it from Jackson. The dog I was holding took an exception to her sudden movement and surged forward, trying to sink her teeth in Loreen's arm. The woman retreated hastily.

"Take that awful thing away from here."

"Gladly," Jackson said, and pulled Douglas back to his feet. He didn't try to resist. He had likely been through this before and knew he couldn't be held long with such flimsy charges against him.

We took the stairs down and were soon at Jackson's car. "Should we take him to the nearest station or the same one they took Lonnie?"

But to my utter bafflement, Jackson released the cuffs and freed Douglas. "Actually, we're not legally allowed to make arrests."

"I could sue you for this," Douglas spat, massaging his wrists as he made his way to the delivery van he had driven here in.

"You can try."

Douglas didn't answer, but just got in the car and drove off with tires spinning.

I didn't understand anything anymore. "Why did you put the cuffs on him in the first place if you can't arrest him?" I asked when we were back in his car.

"It made him easier to handle. And it got the woman to talk." He patted at his jacket pocket where the phone was. "We'd better get this to Thorne."

The dog squirmed in my lap. "I think we have more pressing concerns. Like whose dog is this?"

Chapter Twenty-two

CHERYL SHRIEKED IN DELIGHT when we showed up with the dog. "Who is this, then?" Clearly she had a better eye for dogs than Mrs. Allen. I placed her on Cheryl's desk and put the pink collar she had bought for Pippin/Mac on her. She looked absolutely wonderful in it.

"Her name is Misty Morning." We had dropped by a vet on our way to the agency and had them check her for a microchip, which there had been to our surprise.

"She's three years old, and a border terrier Yorkie mix. She's in very good condition and all her shots are up to date too. And she belongs to Morning Glory shelter in Elizabeth." It was in New Jersey, but under an hour's drive from our office—in good traffic—if you went through the Staten Island.

We assumed that Douglas had stolen her from there when Moreira failed to get Pippin through me. Not that I could easily picture him skulking around the shelter, looking for a correct dog. Maybe he'd sent an underling.

"So chances are you can adopt her."

I told her the story of how we'd got her while she petted the dog, who seemed to be as good natured and as curious as Pippin had been. When I finished, she immediately picked up the phone.

"I'll call there and ask right now."

The speaker was on and Jackson and I listened in as she made the call. "Yes, of course I remember her," the helpful woman with a heavy Jersey accent said at the other end. "She was only adopted this morning. Has something happened to her?"

"She appears to have become lost from her new owner," Cheryl said, her shoulders slumping, and I felt for her. I'd been absolutely certain we'd found a dog for her. "But the microchip only listed you."

"The new owner likely hasn't had a chance to update the info yet. Let me look it up for you." There was a clicking of a keyboard in the background. "The new owner is Jonny Moreira. A very nice young man who was in a great hurry to get exactly that dog for his sister who had recently lost her dog, poor dear. He made a handsome donation to our shelter too."

Jackson and I exchanged amused looks. We wouldn't exactly describe Moreira as nice. Then again, Suzy's mother had used that exact word too, so maybe he appeared different to older women. Or he was good at pretending. And the donation made sense, if he'd wanted to speed things up. You couldn't normally take a dog from a shelter without a waiting period.

"Shall I look for the address?"

"Thank you, but we're private investigators and will find it ourselves." Cheryl hung up and sighed. "I guess I'll look him up."

Jackson smiled. "No need. Moreira works for Craig Douglas. He won't want the dog back. And since she's legally his, the shelter won't be asking for her back either."

"So I can keep her?"

"Absolutely."

She dashed to him and pulled him down to a hearty hug, as if he had given her the best gift of her life. Technically the dog wasn't ours to give, but Jackson was right. Moreira wouldn't want her.

And even if he did, he'd have to fight for it. With Cheryl, by the looks of it. She might even win.

We retired to Jackson's office and Jackson e-mailed the video to Daniel Thorne. He called back a moment later and Jackson put it on speaker.

"That video is excellent. Great work. How much do I owe you?" Jackson named the sum, which made my brows shoot up. It seemed large, considering we'd only spent about an hour on his case, but Thorne accepted it without comment.

"Excellent. And I'll be adding two hundred dollars for finding Mac."

"That's generous of you," Jackson said, making a 'got ya' face at me when I feared he would refuse.

"You've earned it."

Jackson smiled at me when he ended the call. "I believe you can keep the finder's fee."

"Minus your cut?"

"Nah. You've earned the whole."

I most assuredly had. I'd been held at gunpoint for it.

"What's next?"

"We'll go catch Costa."

"Excellent."

He wouldn't escape again.

Jackson drove to Costa's apartment in East New York. "You think he'll be here now, when he wasn't before?" I asked, studying the dark windows of Costa's place. It didn't exactly look like anyone was home.

"We've been through all the other places, and apart from his wife, no one seemed willing to hide him. We'll go to her next if he's not here."

I followed him to the entrance. Jackson pushed the door and this time it opened. His hand went to the gun inside his jacket and I tensed.

"You think there's trouble?" I asked in a low voice when he took it out.

"Yes. Go back to the car."

"No." In this neighborhood there was only one safe place and that was right next to Jackson. To my surprise, he didn't argue when I dug out my pepper spray and followed him in.

The hallway smelled of mold and cigarette smoke, the walls were gray from years of smut and the floor was missing tiles. Narrow steps led up to the next floor and they squeaked under Jackson's weight, so he leaned against the wall to take the load off. I followed the example, even though my skin crawled when I brushed those disgusting walls.

We made it relatively quietly to the next floor. A short, dim corridor led to Costa's apartment door, but there was enough light to see a man crouched before it, picking the lock open. Jackson lifted his weapon and took a two handed aim at the man.

"If you're going to shoot, at least wait until I've picked the lock," Moreira said calmly, not even turning to look.

You could've dropped me with a feather, but Jackson's aim didn't waver. "What are you doing here?" He kept his voice low but firm.

"We told Tracy we'd get Costa." He used my name as if we'd been introduced.

"And I told you we'd handle it," I reminded him, annoyed both because he hadn't believed me and for his familiarity.

Then again, we'd been through extraordinary events together, so I guess we knew each other well enough for him to call me by my first name.

"You can have him once I'm done with him," Moreira said, getting up.

"That's petty of you."

"We can't let little shits jump on our noses."

That's mafia for you.

He pushed the door open, drew out his weapon, and entered the apartment stealthily like a commando. I'd say he owed his training as bodyguard slash mafia goon slash B&E pro to the military. Special ops, by the looks of it.

Jackson and I exchanged baffled glances and followed, although he made me wait by the door while he and Moreira searched the place. It was small, ramshackle, and empty of Costa.

"Fuck." Jackson looked angry. "I was so sure he'd be here."

"Since we're here, we might as well search for his stash," Moreira said.

Jackson gave him a slow look. "I don't have a legal right to do that."

Moreira sneered. "Good thing I don't care about legal rights, then."

We watched in silence as he went through the most obvious places—and the few less obvious ones. "Haven't the police already searched here?" I had to ask.

"Not in the past couple of days."

"And what did you think to do with it if you found it?" But he just shrugged. His unruffled cool aggravated me, so I tried another topic.

"By the way, we gave your dog to our secretary."

This made him pause and look at me. He smiled and I could actually understand why old women thought him nice. Good thing I knew better.

"Yeah? Good. I can send you the paperwork too."

"Okay, this is officially the weirdest house search I've ever attended," Jackson growled. "We're leaving. Including you," he said to Moreira.

"Nothing here anyway."

We returned to the street and the tension between the men returned. "I should have you arrested for scaring Tracy," Jackson said to Moreira. His eyes said that he'd rather punch the guy instead. If he'd still been holding his gun, he might have even used that.

"I already apologized to her," Moreira said, looking squarely at Jackson.

My hand went into my pocket and to the pepper spray I'd put back there. If needed, I'd spray both of them. But as if by a press of a button, the spell that had kept them immobile released, and they both headed to their own directions so abruptly that Jackson was half-way to the car before I thought to move.

Hurrying after him, I was passing the door to the drycleaner's when it opened. I glanced automatically at who was exiting, not really caring, and came face to face with Costa. He was carrying a large laundry bag not unlike the one Jarod had used, only gray. It seemed heavy, so he must have had everything he owned washed.

I paused and he did too. We stared at each other. Then he swerved around and dashed back into the drycleaner.

"Hey!" I didn't think. I just ran after him.

It was a small place and he was faster than me even with the bag. He had already crossed the floor to the back room when I got in. I followed. The old lady at the counter tried to prevent me from getting past her, cursing loudly in her native language—they sounded like curses anyway—when I wouldn't stop.

The small back room opened to the cleaning facilities where two women were working. They barely paused to watch as first Costa and then I ran past them to the backdoor. It opened onto a small lot with dumpsters, old cars, and junk. It was separated from the adjoining lot by a tall wire-netting fence, and I eyed it worriedly, fearing he would climb over it. I'd try to follow, but I most likely wouldn't succeed.

Luckily for me, he ran towards the street instead and I forced myself to go faster, even though I was wheezing already. I wouldn't be able to keep this up much longer. But when Jackson whizzed past me with long strides that ate the distance to Costa with every step, I gritted my teeth and pushed faster. I would not give up the chase.

But I was no match for the men, and by the time I reached the street they'd already disappeared. Breathing heavily, I jogged to the next corner—and could finally pause.

Jackson had Costa on his knees and handcuffed. His gun was out, but it was pointed at Moreira, who was standing in front of them, aiming his weapon at Costa.

"Let go, Moreira," Jackson said with authority. "You lost."

I limped closer and pulled out my pepper spray. I hadn't had a chance to use it once, and this was as good an opportunity as any. I paused by Jackson and pointed the can at Moreira's face, my finger itching to release the spray.

The big man stared at Costa for a few pregnant moments, impassive. He wasn't angry with Costa; this was a task for him, nothing personal. Then he looked at Jackson and lifted his hands in mock surrender, winked at me—the bastard—and turned around, not looking back. Jackson only put his weapon away when Moreira had got into his car.

"And you," Jackson said, glowering at me, "What the hell were you thinking?"

I hadn't, but I wasn't about to admit it. "We got the guy, didn't we? Stop bitching and let's get him away from here."

He shook his head. "You'll be the death of me. I just know it." He pulled Costa to his feet and led him to our car, nodding to me as he went. "Come, I'll show you how the skips are booked. And then we'll definitely call it a week."

I took the heavy laundry bag Costa had dropped when Jackson caught him. It felt lumpy, not at all like it contained clothes. The mouth had become loose, so I'm sure I didn't break any laws when I peeked inside.

The bag was full of money.

"Boss? I don't think we can call it a week just yet."

Epilogue

IT'S AMAZING THE FUSS THAT finding the money created. We had to call the cops, who came in, took Costa and arrested the old woman's son too for hiding the stash—Costa ratted him out. Then we were questioned at the station, as if we'd had anything to do with the crime. It was hours later before we had time for the bail bond formalities. We got a check for two thousand dollars and Jackson gave me half of it. Yay.

There would be money coming from the insurance company of the bank too, for finding Costa's stash, but Jackson said that it would go to keeping the agency solvent. Since it would ensure that I had a job in the future, I didn't mind.

I had my first free Saturday in forever and money burning in my pocket. I should've rushed to the mall at the first light, but I couldn't muster the energy to go shopping. I could barely get out of bed. I'd been running on adrenaline ever since being held at gunpoint, and now I was all out.

So I did what any normal person would do: went to

my parents' and let them fuss over me. It especially helped that Dad said I'd done a good job. I didn't tell him about being held at gunpoint. I'm not an idiot.

But I didn't feel heroic either. I felt at a crossroads. I'd successfully ceased being a waitress, but I wasn't a P.I. yet. I wasn't entirely sure Jackson wanted to keep me even, although he'd said "See you on Monday," as his parting words.

But it wasn't solely about that either. I felt like I couldn't properly start a new life without having closure with the old one. Not the waitressing; I was totally over that. I'd had to come to terms with my divorce.

I would have to go see Scott.

I really didn't want to, but if I was brave enough to face a bank robber, I would be brave enough to do this. Though not brave enough to do it alone. So I put on nice clothes, made-up my hair and face extra carefully, and then forced Trevor to put on some proper clothes too and come with me.

"Are you sure this is a good idea?" he asked when we entered the Irish bar on 18th Street.

"Don't worry. I'll just go and say hello to my ex-husband and ask how he's been these past six years. Nothing dramatic."

The place was jam-packed even though it wasn't a game night, and it didn't take me long to figure out why. On the tiny stage at the end of the bar was a man with a guitar performing to an enraptured audience. We couldn't get very close, but I didn't mind. It gave me a perfect opportunity to just watch Scott in his element.

He was still good. Listening to him brought back all the memories of why I'd fallen so madly for him that I'd left everything to follow him. His voice made me feel like the third sip of whiskey, warm and tingly; he was sexy, and incredibly charismatic. In the packed bar, where he couldn't possibly see me, it felt like he was singing just for me. I leaned against Trevor and simply enjoyed the performance.

When it was over I applauded wildly with the rest of the audience. The crowd began to mill, some to their places or out the door, many towards Scott. I allowed the latter crowd to pull me closer to him. I was increasingly nervous, and I had to keep repeating to myself that this couldn't be worse than being held at gunpoint.

Then the crowd parted before me and he was there. He looked straight at me, but it took him a heartbeat to recognize me. Then he smiled, warm and happy to see me, and I smiled back. Maybe I wouldn't have to seek closure; maybe I could seek reconciliation. We were both different people now and might be able to make it work.

"Hi," he said.

"Hi."

Okay, maybe we'd need more for reconciliation, but it was a start. I was about to ask how he'd been when a leggy blonde with fake boobs came out through the kitchen door, claiming his attention. He reached his arm to her and she wrapped herself around him on his lap, and pulled him into a hot kiss. And he kissed her back.

What the hell?

Acknowledgements

It's not easy to jump to a different genre after years of writing romance, and I couldn't have done it alone. I would like to thank all the usual suspects for making this book happen. My sisters for kindly reading every draft and providing comments. My editor, Lee Burton, for making the language beautiful and checking the obscure facts to make sure they were correct. All the remaining mistakes are mine. And my husband for his patience when the muse wasn't favorable and I wasn't exactly a ray of sunshine. Thank you for vacuuming.

Read a sample of the next
Tracy Hayes adventure:

Tracy Hayes, P.I. and Proud

Chapter One

I was climbing out of a dumpster when I found the body. It was wedged between the wall and the large trash container, and couldn't be seen except from where I was perched. A good thing, then, that I was there.

Mind you, I hadn't meant to be in the dumpster. I wasn't dumpster diving—this time around. I wasn't broke—at the moment anyway—or ecologically aware. I was a P.I.—well, an apprentice of one—and going through people's trash was a viable method for finding evidence, so sooner or later I'd have to do that. But I wasn't here for that either. Based on my experience today, I wasn't looking forward to it.

No, I'd climbed *on* the dumpster in order to reach the bottom rung of the fire escape ladder that was right above it. Being only five-foot-six, I needed the boost. Not that it had been easy to climb on the lid of the dumpster either, but I'd persevered.

Then the damn thing had given up under me, plunging me into the smelly depths. The plastic trash bags had softened my landing, but quite a few of them had broken on impact. There was a wet spot on the bottom of my jeans, and what I hoped were coffee grounds in my sneaker. I really didn't want to know what was clinging from my hair.

Climbing out of the dumpster wasn't any easier than climbing up on it. I'd managed to pull my upper half through the hatch and was taking a small rest, balancing on my stomach halfway in and out—not as comfortable as you might think—when I saw the dead woman. Only the legs were visible from my vantage point, but they were delicate and finely formed, and there were pretty high-heeled slippers on her feet, so I was certain it was a woman.

I froze for a few heartbeats, not entirely believing my eyes. I'd never seen a body before, and I definitely hadn't expected to see one here. Well, not a dead body anyway. I was trailing a cheating husband, and if I'd managed to climb up the fire escape and get a peek through the window, who knows what kind of body I might have seen.

Then again: eww.

More to the point, this wasn't a back yard in a crime-infested slum. This was a respectable neighborhood, and the alley hosting the dumpster was closed in with a tall wire-net fencing and a locked gate. Dead bodies weren't expected here.

Recovering my senses, I dragged myself out of the dumpster, and after some maneuvering managed to drop on my feet without falling or tearing my clothes.

Quite impressive, actually, for a woman with my physique.

I took a quick stock of my appearance, but there wasn't much I could do to improve it. I wiped my hands on the legs of my jeans—no change in their griminess—took off my sneaker to pour out the coffee grounds, picked out the icky stuff from my hair without looking at what it had been—the texture and smell made me think of fish skin—and noticed that I'd lost my butterfly hairclips in the dumpster.

That upset me. I loved those hairclips. I'd paid dearly for those hairclips. I liked how they made my boss give me puzzled looks, as if he was wondering why he had hired a seven-year-old girl instead of a twenty-seven year old woman. But no way was I diving back in to fetch them. I'd sooner drive to Brownsville and buy new overpriced hairclips.

Sighing for their loss, I dug my phone out of my only slightly dirty messenger bag. "I found a body," I said the moment my call was answered.

My boss was silent for a few heartbeats. "Did you call the police?"

"No, I called you. I don't know what to do."

"You call the police. That's what you do when you find a body," Jackson Dean said with a patient tone. He was good with that tone. I heard it often. I'd only begun as his apprentice at Jackson Dean Investigations three weeks ago, and I had a lot to learn.

"I know that. I'm not an idiot, and I have two cops in my family. I called you because I'm not sure if I should be here when the police arrive or not."

He sighed. "Where are you?"

"Somewhere in Gravesend." It was at the southern end of Brooklyn, before Coney Island.

"What the hell are you doing there?"

"You told me to keep on that guy's tail. He came here. I followed."

"And did you do anything illegal that would make it necessary that you're not there when the police arrive?" I had to think about it and he groaned: "Tracy?"

"Well, I'm in this side alley that's closed with a locked gate," I confessed. "But a woman came out of there and she kindly held the gate open for me."

"And where is the body?"

"Behind the dumpster in the alley."

"The closed and locked alley?"

"Yes."

"Okay, I guess you haven't done anything illegal. Call the police. And don't move. I'll come fetch you."

The 61st Precinct wasn't far and it didn't take the first patrol car long to arrive. I was waiting by the locked gate ready to let the police in—and keep everyone else out. Two uniformed officers, one seasoned cop close to retirement and his much younger partner, came over to me, nodded, and then took an involuntary step back.

"Sorry about the smell," I said, embarrassed. "I fell in the dumpster."

"And how did that come about?" the older cop asked with a long-suffering voice.

"I'm a P.I. It kind of comes with the job." I wasn't going to confess I'd been about to climb the fire escape to take a look through someone's window. I was pretty sure that was illegal. Or at least seriously frowned upon.

"Can I see some identification, please?"

I dug out the laminated P.I. ID from my bag. I hadn't had many chances to show it yet, so I felt excessively proud when I gave it to the cop, who studied it closely. In my current state I wasn't sure I matched the photo.

Then again, it was a bad photo.

"Tracy Hayes." He frowned. "I'm not sure I know of Jackson Dean."

"He used to be a homicide detective at the 70th."

That seemed to be good enough for him, because he gave the card back and asked me to show them the body. I took the men to the dumpster and pointed behind it, not looking myself. I really, really didn't want to witness more than the feet I'd already seen.

"Have you touched it?"

"No."

Make that a hell no.

It was dim in the alley, the tall buildings on both sides blocking much of the morning light. The older cop took out a heavy duty flashlight from his belt and leaned against the wall to point the beam at the body. He couldn't get much closer than the feet without moving the dumpster, but it was close enough.

He pulled back, looking ill. "Shit. Was the gate closed when you came?"

"Yes." Sort of.

He sighed and addressed his partner. "Better call this in. Someone's bashed the poor lady's head in." I fought the nausea his choice of words caused. The younger man took out his radio and the older guy gave me a grim look. "Hell of a way to start a Sunday, if you'll pardon my French."

"At least you're not covered in fish entrails."

That made him smile.

He ushered me out of the alley but told me to wait for the detectives, so I leaned against the brick wall outside the fence. People were already gathering to stare, most of them in their Sunday best, having been on their way to church. No one came near me and I didn't wonder it. I reeked.

More patrol cars came, spewing out uniformed cops who began cordoning off the area. I showed them my P.I. card and told them I was the one who found the body, and they let me be.

The forensics team arrived in their van. A man and a woman got out, put on their white disposable overalls, and carried their heavy kit to the crime scene. I watched them work with fascinated interest. I'd never been to a crime scene before and wanted to know everything.

Finally a black Ford Edge pulled over behind the patrol cars, and to my utter delight my brother Trevor exited. When you've found your first body, family was exactly who you wanted to see. Especially if said family member was a homicide detective.

Trevor was four years older than me, half a foot taller, and quite a bit more muscled. He also had nice strawberry-blond hair, and green eyes on a lightly-freckled, manly face, whereas my auburn hair came from a can and my blue eyes from Dad. My more feminine body came from Mom by way of various Brooklyn cafés. I'd worked years as a waitress, and free donuts had been one of the very few perks.

The only perk, come to think of it.

I don't know which of us was more surprised to see the other. "What the hell, Tracy?" He looked more worried than angry when he leaned over to give me a hug, only to pull hastily back. "Whoa. What did you do, bathe in dead fish?"

"I fell into a dumpster."

"Why am I not surprised. I take it was you who found the body, then?"

"Yes." I nodded a greeting at his partner, Detective Blair Kelley, a forty-something tall and commanding black woman, who had come in with Trevor. She nodded back from a safe distance, a small smile on her face.

"So how come you're here?" I asked my brother. "You work in the 70th."

"It's Sunday. We don't exactly keep homicide detectives on call in every precinct."

You learn something new every day.

"Stay put. We'll take a look at the crime scene, then you're going to tell me everything."

"I can't wait."

Made in the USA
Middletown, DE
29 October 2018